T0354833

THE DAISY

Angell Marcella Davis

authorHOUSE®

AuthorHouse™
1663 Liberty Drive
Bloomington, IN 47403
www.authorhouse.com
Phone: 1 (800) 839-8640

Published by AuthorHouse 08/24/2015

ISBN: 978-1-5049-3308-7 (sc)
ISBN: 978-1-5049-3307-0 (e)

Library of Congress Control Number: 2015913744

Print information available on the last page.

This book is printed on acid-free paper.

KJV
Scripture quotations marked KJV are from the Holy Bible, King James Version (Authorized Version). First published in 1611. Quoted from the KJV Classic Reference Bible, Copyright © 1983 by The Zondervan Corporation.

MSG
Scripture quotations marked MSG are taken from THE MESSAGE. Copyright © 1993, 1994, 1995, 1996, 2000, 2001, 2002, 2003 by Eugene H. Peterson. Used by permission of NavPress Publishing Group. Website.

ACKNOWLEDGEMENTS

Nothing is possible without God, so I would like to thank Him first and foremost. Lord, I am forever grateful for the work that you're doing in me. I am not the same person I was in the past and I am excited to be used by you and I will continue on the path that you have for me. I would also like to thank my beautiful daughter, Angelique. Without you in my life, there would be no meaning or purpose. It has always been "me and you against the world." I am very proud of the young woman that you have turned out to be. I love you dearly. To my mom, thank you for all that you do for me and for always praying for me. Thank you to my cousin, Delithia Moore-Turner, for being the first person to purchase my first book "Removing the Painting" and for always being supportive in every aspect of my life. Love you.

Sylvia Mauldin, my best friend since middle school, thank you for always being the one to make me smile and for always being supportive. Antoine Nichols, we've been friends since kindergarten and I can't imagine life without you in it. Thank you for your continued support and love. Thanks to my close friends, Shana Harris and Walter Smith. The two of you have been supportive in every way and thank you for always providing faith-based conversations and genuine friendship to me throughout the years. Thank you for always telling me the truth, even when I didn't want to hear it. Your presence in my life is God-sent and I am truly grateful for you both. Shana, thank you, also, for taking time out to be the first one to read this book before it was published and for sharing your valuable opinion with me. Barbara Taylor, thank you for being my second mother and for always providing the best advice and spiritual guidance. Thank you, Quincy Gibson, for taking time out to read my book before it was published and for assisting me with cutting down some of the messages. I appreciate your support.

Thank you, Bishop Vaughn McLaughlin (Potter's House International Ministries), for allowing me to use parts of your message "He is God of your Broken Places" to use for the fictional character, Pastor Jilah Johnson. Your messages from God and your spiritual guidance have helped me get through some very tough times in my life and I am more than grateful to be a part of your ministry. Thank you, also, to your beautiful wife, Narlene McLaughlin, for her continued support as well.

Special thanks to Edie Jo Mitchell for taking time out of your busy schedule to be the co-editor for me. I really appreciate your second pair of eyes and for your support. Thank you to my good friend and graphic designer, Tyrone Johnson, for designing the cover for me. Your creativity and talent is priceless and I am grateful for all that you contribute to my visions and dreams. Thanks to fellow poet, Travis Rogers, for allowing me to use his poems "My Rib," and "My Favorite Instrument." You are a great poet and I'm happy to publish two of many of your great pieces. Thank you to Mary Osborne for allowing me to use the "A Predetermined Lifespan" part of her article "Stages of a Decaying Flower." Your words fit perfectly with the description of my character's life.

Last, but certainly not least, I would like to thank YOU, my readers, for supporting me and believing in my visions. You inspire me to carry on….thank you all.

PROLOGUE

The truth about relationships remains unseen-
Behind false images that could not have been foreseen.
For all the tears that were shed, for all pain that was bore-
Waking up one day with eyes red and sore.
Wondering what happened to the love once known-
Like a day gone past and the sun that never shown.
Maybe you feel with the mind and no longer with the heart-
Maybe it wasn't really true love from the start.
How can one love someone one day and not the next?
Is it because the virtue of love is one that's perplexed?
To feel a love, yet never feel the depth of that love is a curse-
To lose a love, yet never understand why is even worse.
Manifesting a self love is what should become-
And through it all – it's back to love that we succumb.
If only but one lesson learned.
If only but one soul yearned.

MEMORIAL HOSPITAL MAY 8, 1991

"How long have I been here?" I asked the doctor standing beside my bed. Nothing had been clear to me. I turned my head searching for an answer, and noticed none of my friends or family standing by my side.

"A couple weeks, Mr. Wilkerson, a couple weeks. How are you feeling?"

I tried to discern whether or not the pain was coming from my heart or from the complete emptiness that surrounded me.

I opened my mouth to speak but nothing came out, so I just turned my head and stared out the window. It was a beautiful day outside and I dreaded not being able to run through the trees and lay on the grass the way I used to do. My name is Anthony Trevon Wilkerson. I was born in Miami, Florida on June 7, 1963. I grew up in the heart of the ghetto, searching for a way out. My mother died when my brother and I were too young to remember, and we were abandoned by our father at the same time. We were being raised by our uncle Steve.

Steve Wilkerson was a big man with beady eyes and a bald head. You could always find Steve sipping on a beer in front of the TV. I've never known Steve to ever have a job and he always said he refused to slave for the white man for a small piece of America's dream; a dream that he felt he'd never fully receive. Instead, he sat back and received a check from the government once a month. Uncle Steve felt the welfare checks were owed to him for all the years of suffering our people endured. Although Steve was fun to be around, we spent most of our time at our aunt's house down the street.

My brother Rashawn was four years older than I was. Rashawn Wilkerson Jr., stood 6'3 and weighed 220 pounds and had never cut his hair. Uncle Steve's girlfriend, Pat, would come over every week just to braid his hair. Rashawn and I were always very close because we're all we have in this world. I wondered where he was. Did he not know I was here? Did he not really love me? I was his only brother, why wasn't he here?

As I stared out the window, I noticed the daisies in the front of the hospital's gift shop outside. I always had this fascination with flowers, particularly daisies. When I was a child I would stare at the daisies in my aunt's backyard. Every day the daisies looked different with the change of the seasons until one day the beauty of the daisies just came to a complete halt. It reminded me of life and the way my life has been. I wiped the tears falling from my eyes as I laid there in amazement. Where did I go wrong???

Chapter One

TONY: THE LAST WEEKEND

"Tony, wake up, it's time to get up," yelled my Aunt Tina. Tina Watson was my mother's sister. She had very short hair that she loved to comb back and slick down. She was no more than 5 feet tall and had very huge hips. She had the prettiest caramel complexion and a curved smile. Her teeth were all crooked but somehow she would light up the room with her beautiful grin. Tina had a really heavy voice when she spoke. It appeared that she had been a smoker all of her life but I knew otherwise; Tina would never pick up a cigarette. Tina always liked to tell my brother and I stories about how much our mother Elaine was in love with our father, Rashawn Wilkerson. She would tell us how happy they were when Rashawn Jr. was born and even happier three years later when I was conceived. I've always blamed myself for my mother's death because she died while giving birth to me. The doctors warned her that there would be complications having me and thought it would be wise to abort me. My mother decided against that idea and told her family that Rashawn needed a brother; somehow she knew I'd be a boy. Elaine had decided against an abortion the very day I was conceived. There have been so many times in my life I wished she had made a different choice....

I jumped out of my aunt's bed and looked at the time. I had to be at work by 8:00 A.M. and it was already 7:30 A.M. I worked at Whitters Insurance Companies of Miami. I had just gotten promoted to the main office located in Orlando. My position as a Quality Coach allowed me to befriend all of the Corporate Directors and Managers. I've always tried to network to get my name in front of them all so whenever there were special

1

projects or new training opportunities, I was always considered. This past Friday they gave me a surprise going away party at my job. The biggest surprise was that Lechelle was there. Lechelle was a manager I slept with a few years ago. She was about 4'5 and had curves to die for. She was a dark skinned woman with a really big nose and her hair was usually nappy and uncombed. Often times you would hear several co-workers talking about how ghetto she looked when she came to work. I first met her at a manager's meeting she was facilitating and she stared at me through-out the entire meeting. I pretended not to notice because I didn't think she was much of a sight to look at. However, once she got up out of the chair I found myself drooling. Her body was unbelievable! She stopped me after the meeting, complimented my style of dress and slipped me her business card with her home phone number written on it. After talking to her for a few nights, I invited her to my place and we had sex all night long but the next day I purposely ignored her. I told her I didn't want to see her anymore and she cried and cursed at me. She was angry with me from that point on because she felt used. This is the reason I was nothing but surprised to see her at my party with a goodbye gift. My curiosity ceased when I finally opened the gift; a pair of boxers with the words *I'm an asshole* written on them with a marker.

I always hated Monday mornings because every Sunday night I went to poetry night at the *Lighthouse Club.* The night before I partied all night and drank a little more than usual because I was celebrating the new job I was offered a couple weeks ago at the main office in Orlando. I tried to get my brother Ray to go out with me but he was too busy spending time with his low-down girlfriend Shawna. God knew I hated that girl and I didn't like the fact that she was taking up all of my brother's time. He chose not to go party with me but he promised he would come have drinks with me a day or two before I left and come to Orlando to see me. We'll see if Shawna will allow that or if she will insist on coming along with him. Lord knows I hoped that wouldn't happen. He couldn't even help me move because he had to take Shawna to see her sick grandmother that weekend.

The *Lighthouse Club* was a spoken word poetry club. They played jazz there on certain nights and had live poets on other nights. This club was a normal pick-up spot for me. I'd always serenade the women with a poem or two and then pick which one I wanted to take home. Sometimes I'd even make up a name for myself and create a whole new life for the woman I chose. I could always tell what kind of man a woman was looking for just by the first five minutes of our conversation. For that night I'd become her dream guy and be gone by the morning. I did this for the reason of not having to worry about the woman stalking me or trying to force a relationship on me. I am definitely too young to commit myself to one woman especially with all these women throwing themselves at me. *I am irresistible!*

The night before was a special night for me because it would be my last night at the club for a while and my last weekend in Miami as a resident. I walked into the club with the intention of serenading a beautiful woman and celebrating my promotion with a BANG! I went straight to the bar and ordered a vodka with cranberry juice and sat there while a man dressed in all white read a poem about leaving his past behind. *Uh, sounds like something I wanted to do, leave my past behind.* I wanted to forget about my life here in Miami and start a new one in Orlando. Twenty-eight was the perfect age to start my life all over again. Just as I was smiling at the thought of leaving the past behind, a group of women walked in. One was very beautiful in the face but she was flat as hell when it came to her body and the other two were at least 200lbs. I didn't do the *flat* or the *fat*, unless times were hard and normally with me times were never hard. I searched the room to find that one and alas! There she was; a new and beautiful face. There was a guy sitting there with her and another woman but the guy appeared to be with the other woman. I walked over to her with great confidence.

"You are as beautiful as the setting of the sun." I noticed how beautiful her smile was when I spoke.

"Is that right?" she gracefully asked. I put my finger to her lips and whispered, "Shhh, don't speak, just listen. I'm new in this town and I just came here last month to take care of my dying mother; she has cancer. I've been so lonely since I've been here and I would be so grateful to spend the night with you."

"Oh please, girl I know you're not gonna fall for that lame bull are you?" her girlfriend stated in a snobby tone.

"I'm sorry to hear about your mother, you must be extremely depressed," she replied, ignoring her girlfriend's statement.

"I am, I need to relieve all this stress. By the way, my name is Davante." No one here knew my true name because every time I read a poem I read it as a different character.

"I'm LaQuana, are you a poet?"

"I surely am and I've written a poem especially for you and those beautiful eyes of yours." She smiled a bright smile as her girlfriend shook her head in disgust. The guy at the table excused himself and walked over to the bar which put me at ease since he was such a big dude. I walked over to the host to let him know I would be going on next and hurried back to her table.

"Excuse me Davante, but are you looking for a girlfriend or a one night stand? See, my cousin's not interested in meeting someone just to screw for the night, whether they have a sick mother or not. You understand me? Now you can read all the poems you want and smile all the smiles you want with those beautiful teeth of yours, but if you are thinking about taking LaQuana home tonight then you can forget it."

"Trisha hush! I am a grown woman and I can make my own decisions. I am so sick of you trying to speak for me." LaQuana got up and moved to an empty table and asked me to join her there. I looked at Trisha with a smirk on my face and walked over to the table LaQuana chose to sit at.

"I'm sorry Davante, please don't mind my cousin. She's a little possessive over me and I hate it. Anyways sexy, am I going to hear that poem or what?"

"I've met women like Trisha before, always trying to control what other women do in their lives but don't have control over the things they do in their own life." As she soaked up every word up I spoke, I heard the host introduce Davante. The crowd went wild when they saw that I was performing as Davante tonight. I got up in front of the crowd and in my sexiest voice ever I uttered the words

"This poem is called *My Rib*," and it's especially for LaQuana." I cleared my throat, looked straight at her and began.

"You're as beautiful inside as you are on the outside.

God broke the mold once he made you.

There's no comparison, nor competition.

Everything about you screams brilliance.

You're presence lingers well after you exit.

Full of gifts, God blessed me with the perfect present.

I cherish you and for that I'll cater...

Your personal waiter I'll be.

For that thing you do with your face when you're happy-

Smile....

Ignites a fire within me.

My senses go crazy for you,

You have an exquisite taste.

And your scent is my favorite perfume.

Your voice sings to my soul.

I lose control and can't resist touching you or staring at your flawless temple.

Your beauty exceeds the limitations of outward appearance And our affection isn't restricted to things that are just physical.

Wholesome and virtuous, she praises and worship so I know our union is nothing less than biblical.

There's no doubt in my mind that this perfect gift was made for me.

For God took a rib from me and made you and now I am finally complete."

The crowd went wild as usual and LaQuana was in tears when I sat next to her side.

"That was beautiful."

"Not as beautiful as you are. You wanna get outta here so you can help keep a poor lonely soul like myself busy?" She started reaching for her purse and I smiled in disbelief, *it worked,* I thought.

She stopped me in the parking lot.

"Where are we going honey? My car is parked in the back over there. Am I riding with you or should I just follow you?"

"Please just follow me. I am on call in case my mother needs me so I may have to take off unexpectedly. I was thinking maybe we could go back to my uncle's house and watch a movie. He has a collection of great movies that I just never had time to watch, I would love to watch one with you."

She stood there for a moment, looked around and then back at me. She seemed a little unsure as to what to do. I don't know where else she expected me to take her but when I said my uncle's house her expression changed.

"Well, I guess that's fine. I am not the kind of girl to get naked with someone I just met. I just want you to know that, so don't try anything."

Yeah right. It was 1:00 A.M. in the morning and she was going back to my uncle's house with me, she would definitely be getting naked. I could tell from how anxious she was to grab her purse that she wanted me. I just had to play my cards right, besides, I loved challenges. I walked her to her car, grabbed the keys from her hand and opened the car door for her. She was grinning from ear to ear.

"Whoa! Fine *and* a gentleman, that's hard to find." I agreed, it is hard to find a man as fine as I am and for him to be a gentleman would be a woman's dream come true, unfortunately, I'm just plain ole fine!

We went back to my uncle's place since he was out of town with his bowling league in Daytona Beach for the rest of the week. We had the house all to ourselves. I went straight to Uncle Steve's collection of movies and browsed through them as to make it appear I really did have movie watching in mind.

"What are you in the mood for, comedy, action or romance?" I looked at her in a sensual way when I said the word romance in hopes she would choose the romance, hands on. She walked up behind me and looked quickly through the selection.

"Uh, I've seen just about all these movies already. Do you mind if we just sit and talk? Play some music or something." *Just what I wanted to hear.* I threw in my Marvin Gaye album and dimmed the lights.

"Your uncle has a very unusual place," she said as she looked around.

"My uncle is a very unusual man. He's really into black which explains why everything in this house is black. He's watching over my mother while I went out to relieve my stress. He said he'd page me if there would be a problem or if he had to leave," I lied.

"Would you like something to drink?" I asked.

"Yes, something tall, dark and handsome." Shoot, she was flirting heavy now. I looked at her with a smile on my face when she tried to clean up her remark.

"I mean yes, I would like a tall drink of water," she giggled. After I poured her water I excused myself to the bathroom. I was already excited and felt a small pounding within. I pulled out the wash cloth and wiped myself down to make sure I was fresh and whispered *"you are big and beautiful"* to my manhood.

"Come sit closer to me," LaQuana yelled as soon as I walked back out. She had her legs crossed on the couch while she just stared at me. She was very attractive with her long straight hair and her grayish looking eyes. I found myself entertained by the conquest of trying to figure out if they were really hers or contacts but I couldn't tell. She looked as if she was mixed with Indian and Black, and reminded me of Pocahontas. Her jean mini skirt hugged her hips and thighs so tight that I wished I was a piece of fabric on her skirt.

"So how long have you been writing poetry? I have tried to write it myself from time to time. I'll let you hear one of mine if you read one of yours to me right now."

I just wanted to get it on. I could tell she wanted to as well so I didn't know where this *'let's talk for a while'* mess was coming from but if that's what she had to do to make herself feel less of a hoe then it was fine with me. Maybe if I enticed her mind with another poem then she would be ready to give it to me. I sat there in silence for a quick second trying to think of one of my shortest poems, I cleared my throat and proceeded.

"So much depends upon a single star, facing the whole world in complete darkness – ALONE."

She released a big sigh.

"That was great! I loved it, short and sweet. Ok, I don't usually let people hear my poetry but I feel so comfortable with you. Are you ready?"

"Shoot."

"Ok, here it goes. I see the world and the people in it and my soul begins to cry. Children abducted, buildings destructed, lives interrupted, makes me wonder why. I never thought watching the news would break my heart, war going on for thousands scorn, families torn apart. Serial killer on the loose, students involved with their teachers. Women drowning their kids. Kids molested by their preachers. I never thought the world today would bring my heart such pain. I never thought the world today would be the reason for this rain. Hearts have been broken from time to time. Only problem is, today the heart is mine."

I was very impressed with her words so I just sat there speechless and smiled at her.

"Well, what did you think?" She waited anxiously to hear my response.

"Wow, those were really deep thoughts. I feel the same way sometimes. Great work." Even though I would've enjoyed talking more with her and finding out what her views were on world issues, I really didn't want to get to know her in that way. I moved closer to her and started to rub her legs. Just as she was about to say another word, I cut her off with a long wet and passionate kiss.

I tore her clothes off right there on the couch.

"Wait, do you have a condom?"

Condom? Heck no! I stopped suddenly in disgust and thought frantically for a second. I knew Uncle Steve had to have a condom somewhere. I ran upstairs and roamed through his drawers until I ran across a half empty pack of condoms. Perfect. I rushed downstairs, showed her the condom and dreaded putting it on. I don't want any kids but I hate wearing those rubber things because it takes away all the pleasure. The majority of the time I never wore condoms, I'd just pull out but I never argued if someone asked for one.

The sex was absolutely incredible despite the constant scratching she managed to do to my back and the occasional *"wait, that hurt"* screams. After we were all sweaty and out of breath I stared at the ceiling trying to figure out how I was going to get this girl out of my house; I was ready for her to leave. I went to the living room to call Rashawn and told him to page me so I could see if my pager was working. I knew I could've paged myself but I wanted it to go off while I was in bed with her. I wouldn't dare tell him the real reason because he definitely wouldn't have done it.

"Man, why are you so worried about your pager working this time of the night? You need to buy you a cell phone when you get to Orlando. It's 2:40 in the morning! Hurry up and hang up so I can page you back." I ran back into the bed with LaQuana and waited impatiently for my pager to go off. RaShawn waited a long dreadful 5 minutes before he actually sent me a page. When my pager beeped, I looked down at it and then jumped out of bed.

"What's wrong baby?" LaQuana looked so concerned.

"That was my uncle paging me 911! That's our code when he thinks my mother may not make it. I've got to go. Hurry! Get dressed." She offered to go with me but I insisted my mother didn't want anyone else around other than family. I walked her to her car and kissed her good night.

"Will you call me?" she asked in an uncertain tone as she wrote down her number.

"Of course, as soon as I get home," I drove off immediately with a smile on my face.

Aunt Tina helped me gather most of my things the rest of the week and she even paid for the moving truck for me. She felt responsible for me and wanted to make sure I made it to Orlando in one piece so she insisted that Uncle Steve accompany me and the moving guys down there. Aunt Tina had always been protective of me since I was the youngest and I always ended up getting into trouble. I remember when I was a little boy she insisted that I played outside in front of her apartment as opposed to going to the playground with the other kids. One particular day, Ray and all his buddies headed to the corner store and then up to the local gym to play basketball. I kicked the ball around outside her apartments for a while and started to get angry that I couldn't hang with my brother and his friends or even go to the playground with my friends. So I decided to teach her a lesson and went to the playground anyway. I was at the playground for about ten minutes before I saw Aunt Tina getting out of her car. She was carrying this big black belt in her hand and all my friends looked at me with an '*oh oh you're in trouble*' look.

I ran to greet her in hopes of buttering her up.

"Aunt Tina, thank goodness you're here. I came to get my homework assignment from Al."

"Homework assignment? Well, where is it?" she seemed to be looking right through me as I tried to stick with my lie.

"Well, turns out I don't have any. I thought we did so I came on over here to ask Al and he broke the news to me that there was none. I was just about to head back."

"Didn't I tell you not to leave the front?" She was pissed off at me and I noticed myself constantly eyeing that belt she held tightly in her hand. There were about five of my friends at the playground, Ray, his friends, and about eight more kids there I didn't know. I was trying my best to not get embarrassed in front of them.

"Yes, ma'am you did. I know you tell me how important homework is so I wanted to make you proud of me and find out on my own about my homework assignment."

"If you were paying attention in class then you would know what your homework assignment was, Tony."

Hmm, she had a point. *If I could just get her back in the car then I would be fine*, I thought. I didn't really care that I had to get a whipping, I just didn't want to get one in front of my friends. Right when I was going to add more to my lie, she started walking over to Al. I just stood there and watched her speak to Al as he shook his head several times at questions being tossed at him. I thought about running to the car but I couldn't move. I had been busted. Aunt Tina told me that not only was I in trouble for leaving without letting her know where I was but I was in even more trouble for lying to her. Next thing I knew I felt my butt burning. She whipped me so hard with that belt that I felt pee running down my legs. Several kids I didn't know were laughing while others, along with my friends, watched as they shook their heads.

My lesson was learned. Since then I have never lied to Aunt Tina or thought I would teach her a lesson again. Anytime I even thought about lying to her I thought about that day in the playground. I was grateful to have her though; she had always been the mother we always needed. She would've had us living with her when my mother died, but at that time in her life she was with an abusive husband who beat her every time he got drunk. Ray even tried to help her one time but the bastard just punched him in the stomach and continued to beat Aunt Tina. That incident was the one that made her finally get up the nerve to leave him. Aunt Tina just couldn't stand the fact that he had the guts to hurt her nephew.

"Tony, don't you get up there getting one of those Orlando girls pregnant, you hear?" I looked at her like she had bumped her head.

"Lady, I am twenty-eight years old. Do you see any children running around here? No, you don't. Do you know why? Because I don't want any so don't you worry your pretty little head off."

"Now don't get me wrong boy, I want you to have a youngster. I just want you to have it with a nice decent young lady who you will marry and settle down with. Lord I don't think I'll ever see the day when you will settle down. Ever since that fast little girl Earlene broke your poor little heart when you were eighteen you have been just ridiculous with the women, Tony. You can't make all these women suffer for something some silly young girl did nearly ten years ago. There are some good women out there who would love to have you as their man and they will treat you like the King you are but you just won't give them the chance."

"Auntie stop it now, quick preaching at me. I just haven't found the right woman, that's all."

"Well, if you start going to church and stop being up in these clubs every weekend then you could find the right woman. And give the woman a chance Tony, you don't give them a chance to win your heart. You are too darn old to be acting like a player, too old."

"Auntie, you're fussing at me again. What's gotten into you lady? I'm looking for a woman who look and act just like you but you know you are one of a kind so it's just so hard to find." I winked at her and she managed to smile through that cringed up face she held.

"Boy, you are a mess. I just want you to know what true love is before you are gone."

"I know, don't worry. And why are you always bringing up Earlene? She was with me over ten years ago, Auntie I've had girlfriends since then. Have you forgotten about Karyn and Stacey?"

"No, how could I forget about them poor dear women you destroyed? Karyn was a sweetheart, and for the whole two years y'all were together you ran around town with every tramp you could find. It's a wonder she didn't leave you sooner than she did. And Lord help Stacey, she loved you with all her heart. She was probably the best woman you ever had. She had her Masters Degree in Education and was one of the best teachers at that college down the street. I was so happy when y'all moved in together and

I thought she would be the one you settled for. She was just so in love with you and you did that girl wrong Tony, sleeping with her best friend right in the bed y'all shared every night. If I would've caught y'all in my bed like she did then I would've killed you both and pleaded temporary insanity, thank God she didn't! You made that girl have a nervous breakdown and move out of town and she gave up her job and everything. I still haven't forgiven you for that."

I just sat there while she lectured me, I was used to hearing this from her so I normally just sat there and let her speak but this time I didn't have the patience or the time. Orlando was waiting and I had to finish getting things together.

"Auntie, I'm sorry but I got to get going. I promise you I will try to find the girl of my dreams in Orlando and I won't hurt her."

She smiled and I kissed her goodbye. Look out Orlando – here I come!

Chapter Two

RAVEN: THE WAIT

I'm sitting here staring out the window. I've been sitting here since 7:00 P.M. and it is now 9:00 P.M. and still nothing. Terrance had not called nor come home. I don't know how much longer I can deal with all of this. What happened to our vows we made to one another two years ago? What happened to our happy home we planned?

My name is Raven Sinclair. I was born on February 7, 1963 in Orlando, Florida. I've been married to Terrance Sinclair for two years and we've been together for three. We had the best marriage for the first year and a half. We did so much together and spent every waking hour looking into each other's eyes. We cherished every moment we shared. But for the past couple of months he's been coming home later and later, and once he didn't even come home at all. The nerve of him! He claimed he caught a flat and his friend Bill came to pick him up. Bill then drove him back to his house but refused to take Terrance home. Miraculously, the phone had been disconnected at Bill's house and Terrance's cell phone battery died. Imagine that, he must think I have the word *stupid* written on my forehead.

I pulled out my journal and decided to write a poem to take my mind off of this nonsense. I've been a poet since I was a child. Every time I entered the poetry contests in school I always won first place. Writing seems like the only way to express how I feel, especially lately since I've been feeling so lonely. It's a shame that I have a husband but I spend more lonely nights now than when I was single. I have many journals full of poetry I've written throughout my marriage and my life but tonight I was starting a brand new one.

Entry Number 1:
"Sometimes-
In the midst of all my darkest fears,
In the center of all my deepest desires,
All my craziest dreams...
Sometimes-
Through all my trials and tribulations
All my heartaches and pains.
Sometimes-
When I'm down and out.
When I'm sad and blue.
When my sunshine turns to rain.
Sometimes-
A sense of relief comes over me-
A sense of freedom overwhelms me-
Sometimes-
Through all the despair and the loneliness
that I sometimes feel.
Through all my tears and all my frustration.
I search deep inside my soul-
I reach deep into my heart –
And I suddenly become – LOVE!!!"

I met Terrance three years ago on my way to *The Millennium*. I was supposed to meet my best friend Shyla there for a couple drinks and our normal Saturday night man hunting. We usually met at *The Stage* downtown but we've been hearing a lot about this new club for a couple of weeks so we decided to check it out. After circling the strip several times, I was just about to give up when a black Mercedes with tinted windows pulled up next to me. *I hope this isn't a maniac, but here goes nothing*, I thought. I blew my horn a few times and when the windows went down I was blown away by the driver.

He was a handsome light skinned man dressed very professional wearing a gray suit and a gray and white tie. He had a low haircut with curly hair, some pretty bushy eyebrows and a million-dollar smile. At first my mind went blank but I quickly regained my composure and spoke.

"I'm sorry to bother you sir, but do you know how to get to *The Millennium?*" I quickly glanced in the mirror to make sure I was presentable and then he replied.

"I'm on my way there now, follow me."

What? Am I underdressed? I hesitated for a second as he made a left turn and then I thought *oh well* and went ahead and followed him. When we pulled into the parking lot I pulled out my cell phone to call Shyla so she could meet me outside but her cell phone was turned off. "Darn!" I said. I didn't realize how packed the place would be. It was going to be hell finding her in that crowd.

"Excuse me," I heard a voice yell and an annoying tapping on my window. I turned around to see the handsome man in the Mercedes standing by my car. I rolled down the window.

"Yes?"

"Did you plan on going in or are you just gonna party out in the parking lot?" I just smiled and got out the car.

"My name is Terrance, and what might your name be, my queen?"

Queen huh? I like the sound of that.

"I'm sorry. My name is Raven and thank you for being so kind. I'm here to meet my girlfriend but this place is so crowded. I don't know if I'll be able to find her."

We started walking towards the entrance when he suddenly stopped in his tracks, looked at me and smiled.

"It really is extremely crowded tonight. I just came back from a Music Seminar in Georgia and I wanted to come get a drink before I headed to the house. How 'bout finding another spot to go to so we can get to know each other a little better?" he stared at me nervously as he awaited my answer. *What to do? What to do?* I would be nuts to go off with this guy I just met and just leave Shyla hanging, although she's done it to me millions of times before.

"Well, how 'bout we just sit in the car and talk? I really don't know you well enough to go anywhere with you and plus I don't want to just leave without seeing my friend." I looked around the parking lot frantically for her car.

"I suppose I can go a little longer without a drink, besides, it's well worth it." He looked me up and down and let out an *"ooh"* as we headed back toward his car. We sat in his car for about two hours talking. As he talked about his three sisters and two brothers, I gazed into his eyes. He had the prettiest eyes I've ever seen. They were just a normal dark brown color but there was something sexy about them and I was a sucker for pretty eyes. The big dimples in his cheeks made my heart tremble as I tried to pay attention to the words he spoke. Somehow he seemed to do most of the talking and I enjoyed listening to his deep, unadulterated voice. I told him about my aspirations of publishing my own poetry book, and also about my drawn out career at one of the biggest mortgage companies in Orlando. He seemed more interested in the fact that I was a writer. He suggested I write a couple songs for some of his groups at the studio he owned. That thought was a wonderful one, but I didn't want to get carried away with talking about future plans, I just met the guy!

"Recite a poem for me," he requested. I hesitated for a moment until I saw that gorgeous smile of his. I cleared my voice, looked dead in his eyes and began.

"The name of this piece is called *All in Time*," he smiled as I continued.

"So many times I want to hold you, but you're too far behind. So many times I want to see you, but suddenly I'm blind. So many times I want to tell you how much I care. So many times I want to touch you but you're not there. I want you to know the dream I hide inside, so many times you see a smile but my heart hears a cry. I want you to promise that you'll always be there for me, so many times you see happiness but my heart knows I'm lonely. The time will come when the sun will finally shine, we'll have to wait but it'll happen... all in time!"

When I finished the poem he stared at me and didn't say a word. He just leaned over and gave me the softest, most romantic kiss I've ever known. I felt warm inside as I pictured us walking down the aisle in holy matrimony. It was a far-fetched reality but that's how I felt when I looked at him. Shyla had completely slipped my mind when I glanced out the window and saw her walking towards a gray Cadillac with a fine dark skinned brotha. I got out the car and signaled for her to come to me.

"What happened to you Miss Lady?" she asked.

"I'm so sorry girl. It was so crowded up in there, a sista just chilled out here with that fine specimen of a man in the car." I pointed at the Mercedes parked behind us as I smiled from ear to ear.

"Girl, you see I didn't miss you, I'm going home with that fine man over there." I looked over at the guy, then at her and shook my head.

"You be careful child and have fun." I said, knowing she would. Shyla stared over in Terrance's direction and stated, "Do him right girl, he's cute."

"I'm not going to *do* him at all but I'll get to know him better, something you should be doing with your guy." Shyla stared at me in disbelief.

"You are much better than I am 'cause I'd do him in a second. Well, let me go and I'll call you later with the details, bye Raven." Shyla ran back to her date and I spent the rest of the night talking to Terrance.

Terrance and I dated for two months before I actually started having undeniable feelings for him. We spent every day together and when we didn't see each other, we talked for hours on the phone. The biggest memory that I've always kept in my heart was the night he proposed to me nine months into our relationship. We had dinner at The Top, a restaurant located on the twelfth floor of a business that over looked all of Orlando. The sun was setting and the sky was a magnificent orange and blue. After dinner we went for a walk. It was a beautiful night and the breeze was warm and soothing as we walked hand in hand. When we arrived to his place, he pulled out champagne glasses and a bottle of Moet. After he poured the champagne in the glasses, he kneeled down on one knee.

"Raven, I've never known beauty until I looked into your eyes. I have never known love until the day I met you. My life would be meaningless without you in it forever. Raven, will you do me the honor of becoming my wife?"

I screamed with great shock.

"Yes, yes, yes!"

The phone rang and interrupted my thoughts as I jumped from the window pane, hoping it was Terrance.

"Hello?"

"Yes, is this Raven Sinclair?"

"Yes, it is. May I ask who's calling?"

"This is Terrance's girlfriend Nicole. Don't be messing with my man or I'll find you and you'll regret it." My heart froze, this couldn't be happening! Not Terrance, my husband and my best friend. As I sat in momentary silence with disbelief, I suddenly heard a burst of laughter.

"Child, I got you good huh? Calm your butt down, this is Shyla girl." I was fuming by that time.

"Shyla, that junk wasn't funny, goodbye," and I hung up. I was furious at her! How dare she play with me like that knowing I was sitting there frantically awaiting my husband's arrival. The phone rang again but I knew it was Shyla calling back so I let my machine pick up. After the beep I heard Shyla apologizing and pleading for me to call her back. I ignored the message and sat in the corner.

Shyla was my best friend. We met in the ninth grade when we were both new to high school. She was a little weird with her dark clothes and dark lipstick she wore everyday but I got used to it. She was always kinda fast when it came to the boys and she used her beauty as a way to overpower them. Shyla Rene Stevens was a beautiful twenty-nine year old manager and part-time model. When she was a full time model, she traveled all over the world modeling and was featured in over a dozen magazines. Now she was a manager at the mortgage company I worked for and she still took pictures from time to time. Men drooled over her long black hair, slanted eyes, full lips and high yellow skin. She had this grace about her that overwhelmed the most confident man. Shyla was what men would call a gold digger. Her house was draped with beautiful furniture, entertainment centers, and fine china that some man bought for her. If she couldn't get money from a man, she'd just use them for sex, which she loved dearly. There had been times when I was afraid for her life when she'd go on her occasional hoe hopping, which is what she liked to call it. When Shyla went hoe hopping, she'd sleep with two different men in one night and occasionally at the same time.

Once we were at a male revue party at one of our girlfriend's houses on New Year's Day some years back. There were two strippers at the party flopping their bulges all in our faces, rubbing oil all over the dramatically screaming women and letting the women take liquor shots off of their body. Shyla took about five shots that night along with the other drinks she sipped on from time to time. I was never really into the strip tease thing so my entertainment came mostly from watching the women act a fool and give these men all their hard-earned money. I never gave money because I worked too hard. Shyla got pretty wild whenever she went to these type of parties and I would always try to get her to slow down but each time you'd hear her say, "Raven, quit being so lame. Leave me alone."

I would feel hurt and offended each time. I knew she would act wild when she was drunk but she also acted like that when she wasn't drunk. This one particular party I found myself dragging her by the hair and driving her home. She was half naked, clothes torn off her and was so drunk she could barely stand. The worst part about that night was when she threw up all in my car. It took me four months to get that awful smell out.

I often wondered why I even hung with her! We didn't have anything in common when it came to men. The wildest thing I've ever done in my life was sleep with my teacher when I was a freshman in college. Sometimes I wondered how that ended up happening but I just couldn't control my desires. English was one of my favorite subjects so I was looking forward to taking English 101. On the first day of class, I walked in only to find this handsome man sitting behind the desk. All the girl students were smiling from ear to ear when he introduced himself.

"Hello class, my name is Eric Boston. I am your professor for English 101. I am here to assist you so don't hesitate to ask me for help."

He was a dark-skinned man who appeared to be in his forties. He had a small bald spot at the top of his head that he tried to cover with the surrounding hair but despite that, he was still fine. Maybe our hormones were just flaming and right around that time any man looked good to us but all the girls snickered and giggled anytime he spoke. After a month I managed to become his top student, always turning in my essays a day early and being the first to answer any question he asked. Every day after class Eric made small talk with me and if I wasn't mistaken, he was flirting with me as much as I was flirting with him. I was nineteen at the time and I knew it was against the rules to date my college professor but I didn't care. I wanted him. I went home at night fantasizing about what it would be like to be with him. I never thought it would actually happen.

I made sure I dressed provocatively each time I went to class. When I became ill in the winter time, I missed two days but I made sure I called Eric for any missed assignments. When I was on the phone with him, I told him my birthday was coming in a few months and I would be twenty.

"You will be almost legal, huh?" he teased.

"Yeah, almost! But good thing I'm still a mature woman. Hey, do you think you can bring me a copy of the assignment I'm missing? I'd hate to be too far behind."

"As much as I'd love to, you are contagious and I can't afford to get sick. How about we spend some time together after class when you're all better to catch up on everything?"

"I'll be looking forward to it." I tried to say that in my sexiest voice ever. There was complete silence on the phone and I was wondering if he was looking forward to it as well, and then he broke the silence.

"Is that right? When did you say your birthday was?"

"February 7th, are you going to get me something?"

I heard him start to talk to someone in the background and I could tell he was in a hurry to get me off the phone all of a sudden.

"Raven, let me go. I hope you feel better and thanks for calling."

I sat there listening to the dial tone. I got an A in his English class but I found out he was also teaching Literature so I made sure I registered for that class for next semester. Right before the end of that semester I wanted to make sure that he would always remember me. I went to the Elegance Engraved store and picked out this beautiful gold coin clock and I had Eric's name engraved on it. I wrapped it and gave it to Eric, making him promise not to open it until the last day of class. I received a phone call from him that evening. He thanked me for the lovely and extravagant gift I got him. He was really surprised and impressed all at the same time. As I was telling him I registered for his next class, he asked me if I wanted to get with him Saturday to help him develop a group experiment for the class.

"Sounds like a plan to me. Is it possible for you to come to my apartment?" I asked.

"Sure, I'll be there around 1:00 P.M."

Saturday came as slow as molasses and I was more nervous about being alone with him in my apartment than I'd ever been in my life. I was so infatuated with this man that I was afraid I wouldn't be able to keep my cool. Saturday at 1:00 P.M. sharp, I heard a knock at my door. I had spent the entire morning cleaning my small apartment and was exhausted. When he walked in, he looked very professional and got right down to business.

"Here are a few ideas I had for group projects. You did so well in my English class that I would love to get your input on the best route to go with these projects." He gave me a list of ideas and I slowly reviewed each one. After I gave him my proposal on the best group project, he acted as if he was about to leave.

"I know you're not about to leave, I want you to stay."

He sat down on the couch and just smiled nervously, perhaps he was feeling the same anxiety I had been experiencing all morning. He began to ask me questions about what I did for my birthday and I told him how I just went to dinner and a movie with Shyla. There were weird pauses between our small talk but we managed to keep our composure. He then began to tell me about the Literature class I registered for and the essay that would be due within the first few weeks of the class.

I sat so close to him that our legs were touching. He didn't seem to mind as he spent the next few minutes reviewing the Literature book and explaining what I should expect once class started. While I had my head down looking through the book, I noticed that Eric had stopped talking mid-sentence. When I looked up, he kissed me. Before I knew it we were naked and had sex right there in the living room. I just couldn't believe what was happening. Afterwards, there was an awkward silence as I just stared at him and smiled. We sat and talked for about an hour after that and he continued to throw in the "please don't tell anyone about this" plea from time to time. I promised I wouldn't. When he left, I spent the rest of the afternoon in la la land dancing and singing around the house as if I were a little child.

For the following six months we continued to see each other secretly, mostly on Saturdays at my place. It was exciting being with him and no one knowing about it. One night Eric got a hotel for us and gave me my first romantic encounter. He had rose petals on the sheets and gave me my first real massage with some strawberry sensual oil. He ran a bath for me and I laid there soaking and relaxing for almost an hour because the water was so soothing that I decided to stay in a little longer than usual. I dried myself off and walked into the bedroom where I found Eric talking on the phone. As soon as I walked in he put his finger to his lips telling me to be quiet. I then realized he was talking to another woman. I didn't really know how to feel as I just stared at him in disbelief. After telling this woman how much he loved her, he hung up and started talking to me as if nothing had happened. When I asked for an explanation, he stated that he forgot to mention to me that he and his girlfriend hadn't broken up as of yet but he was planning on breaking up with her soon. Needless to say, I ended the affair that night. It was truly an encounter I kept in my memory bank, but only the good times. I kept the secret of dating him from everyone, even Shyla. She wondered what I did on those Saturdays I couldn't hang out with her but I always made up some wild excuse. But that night, I revealed it all to her over a carton of ice cream and a bucket of tears.

It was 10:30 P.M. and Terrance was supposed to be home at 5:00 P.M. when he got off of work. I paced the floor looking for something that could occupy my time. I got on my knees and prayed that God would bring him home safely. One of Terrance's main problems with me was the fact that I got saved about six months ago. I started going to church with my cousin periodically but one Sunday I found myself at the altar giving my life to Jesus and begging him to forgive me of all of my wrongs in my life. That same day I came home and tossed out all of our porn collection and sex toys. I explained to Terrance how none of that stuff was of God and he threw a fit. He didn't talk to me that entire week. I started going to church every Sunday after that and pleaded for him to come with me but he always refused. Being saved was difficult for me because I thought I would be changed overnight. I still had my sinful thoughts at times but the difference was that I felt convicted anytime I did things or even thought about doing things that didn't fall in line with God. My pastor told me that being saved would be a process. He said I wouldn't just start speaking in tongues and living holy overnight. I was enjoying this newfound love I found for my God but I felt bad that my husband refused to even try God. Terrance was enjoying the devil too much.

I got off my knees, grabbed my journal and began to write:

Entry Number 2:

I have wept yet I have wept alone, for loneliness has taken control of me. I have had pain yet I hurt alone, for loneliness has taken control of me. I have feared yet I fear alone, for loneliness has taken control of me.

Loneliness has claimed me for its own; I now belong to him. I try to find another but I keep coming back to him. He has taken control of my every thought. He has told me "I am Loneliness and you are ME!

I cooked pork chops, macaroni and string beans as soon as I got home from work, wanting him to come home to a nice home cooked meal. I called his cell phone several times but he did not return my calls. Though I knew it was all in God's hands, I found myself worrying about him laying hurt somewhere. I wouldn't know what I would do without him. I held my pillow close as my worst fear came to mind. I also feared he might possibly be with someone else. Every night before bed he turns his phone completely off, which stirs up curiosity on my end. I felt in my heart that he was fooling around but I just needed hardcore evidence to support my gut feelings. I knew it started to rain outside because I could hear the raindrops hitting my window. I felt myself dozing off in the corner of my bedroom....

Chapter Three

TONY: THE MOVE

We had been moving all day. The movers were in the kitchen laid out on the floor. It had been eighty five degrees the whole time we were unloading and I felt a little dehydrated.

"Boy, this sure is a nice apartment. I might pack my things up and move in, Boy." I stared at my Uncle Steve with a *yeah right* look on my face. Uncle Steve knew I enjoyed my freedom and privacy and he also knew I thought he was a lazy bum and I wasn't having that.

I was overwhelmed with exhaustion and hunger. I planned to order pizza once everyone had left because for some reason I just wanted to be alone in my apartment.

"Uncle Steve, thanks for all the help. I'll unpack the boxes myself; I just really need some sleep."

"Boy, you go to sleep, I'll sit here on this here furniture you just bought, break that sucka in, watch a little TV." Uncle Steve just didn't get the picture. He plopped down in my recliner, kicked his shoes off and grabbed the remote control.

"Boy, this TV is not coming on. Didn't you just buy this here TV?" I looked at him in humor as he looked like the original couch potato.

"It's not plugged in and the cable guy won't be out till a few days from now." At that moment the movers came in with the papers for me to sign. The job paid for my relocation fees so all I had to do was verify they moved everything like they were supposed to. As soon as they left I turned and looked at the stiff stretched out on my recliner.

"You got something to eat? I've been moving this here mess of yours all day, I'm hungry. Order something to eat and come have a little talk with your Uncle Steve." I started to ask him to just leave and grab something on the way out but since he did help me move I figured the least I could do was feed him. I borrowed his cell phone and ordered a pizza and a two liter coke. We sat there and talked about the old days back when Uncle Steve thought he was a player by having two girlfriends and they lived right across the street from each other. I laughed as I reminded him of the lies he had me telling them when he was on the verge of getting caught up. We sat there for hours and talked about everything from politics to movies. In the middle of us laughing about his girlfriend Pat falling out of her chair when they went to dinner, Uncle Steve suddenly got serious.

"Tony, you are my favorite nephew. I just want you to know I am proud of you. You have made me proud." I smiled at him and looked around my apartment at the millions of boxes everywhere; it was time for him to go.

"Oh yeah, I just remembered Pat said she needed you back home uncle, something about a fight she wanted to order for you tonight," I lied. I knew he was a huge boxing fan.

"A fight? Well, I gotta be going son. I'll call you when your home phone gets turned on." He heard the word fight and you would've thought they were giving away a million dollars how fast he jumped up.

"Bye Uncle Steve."

I closed the door behind him and released a sigh of relief. The apartment was quite huge with marble floor throughout the living room. There were two bedrooms, one in which I would make an office. There was a big screened-in patio where I imagined myself relaxing on and enjoying the beautiful weather. I had just gotten some burgundy silk sheets to go on the new bedroom set I just bought. I made sure all my furniture was new because I wanted to have that *new* feeling for everything. I sat on my leather couch and smiled. *Mr. Anthony Wilkerson: Assistant Manager of Whitters Insurance Companies of Orlando*, imagine that. I had been a Quality Coach at the insurance company in Miami for almost five years but I did every job in the company and learned everything I needed to learn. When I applied for this position in Orlando, it was on a night where I was tired of my repetitive life and never really once thought I'd even be considered for the position. My manager gave me such a great recommendation that they called me for an interview the same day they talked to her. Imagine my surprise when I got the phone call.

There was a skinny white woman waiting to greet me when I had the interview. I was quite nervous, I must admit. I hoped the person interviewing me would be a woman so I could use my charm to get the position. The skinny white woman handed me some forms to fill out while I waited. I sat there in anticipation as I stared at the clock. The interview was scheduled for 9:00 A.M. and it was going on 9:15 A.M. I was getting impatient because I hated to wait.

"Mr. Wilkerson, please follow me, they're ready for you now."

When I walked in the conference room, there were three people in there waiting for me. Two were men, *darn*. One of the men had dark black hair, Italian maybe, and he wore glasses and an expensive looking watch. He was wearing a nice expensive looking gray suit and a crooked intimidating smile. The other man looked to be in his late fifties and wore a dark blue suit and held his stare at me when I first walked in. The woman was a black woman to my excitement. She definitely wasn't a candidate for beauty queen but she looked like a million bucks. I smiled, shook everyone's hand and proceeded to sell myself. At the end of the interview, they were eating out of the palm of my hand and grinning from ear to ear as I was getting up to leave. I felt comfortable with them and the more I talked about their company, the more I wanted that job.

As I reflected back on my interview, the phone started to ring. *Gosh, who was calling me already? I told Uncle Steve my home phone wouldn't be on till next week.*

"Hello?"

"May I speak with Anthony Wilkerson please?"

"Speaking, may I ask who's calling?"

"Yes, my name is Sheena Harris. I'm your trainer over at Whitters. I was calling to change your start time. You're supposed to start work in a few weeks at 8:00 A.M. but I need you to come in at 7:00 A.M. on that day instead. Would that be a problem?"

"Whew! Not at all! I thought you were telling me I couldn't start at all," I sighed. Sheena giggled.

"Now why would I do a thing like that? I've heard a lot of great things about you and I look forward to meeting you."

"Same here Sheena, same here. Have a blessed day, goodbye."

I walked over to my window and stared outside. There were so many people walking hastily in the streets. I stayed on the first floor and it seemed like they could just walk up to my window and look in had I not bought my blue shades. I knew no one here but I really wanted to go out and see the city, even if I did get lost. I looked around my apartment and saw all the boxes that needed to be unpacked. I had a long night ahead of me so the sight-seeing would have to wait.

I finished unpacking everything at 1:00 A.M. Saturday morning.

Ring. The phone startled me.

"Hello?"

"Yes, may I speak to Jany?"

"Jany? You have the wrong number"

"You sure?" she asked.

I wanted to say *look old lady, I told you Jany don't live here, this is Romeo Tony's crib now,* but I decided against it.

"Yes ma'am, I'm sure."

I grabbed my notebook and sat down on the window pane in the front room where I stared at the skyline of Orlando, it was beautiful. I opened it and began to write:

'When the city is surrounded by darkness and filled with lights so bright and beautiful, I love to stare at its beauty and imagine. I like to imagine a world where the reality of peace is just as beautiful as my imagination of peace. A world full of dreams and hopes, but when the city lights disappear, reality appears. All the city crimes, city costs and city tears, city worries, forbidden dreams and forgotten years. Reality.'

I passed out with the pen in my hand. When I woke up the next morning I picked up the phone to call my brother Ray.

"Ray, I'm finally here in Orlando. It's great! When are you gonna come see me?"

"Man, you act like you miss me already. I got some things planned with my woman this weekend but maybe next weekend. Are you feeling any better?"

Four weeks ago I came down with an unusual cold. It lasted for almost two weeks. I had to take my vacation days in bed. I had awful fevers during the night and when I coughed it felt like I was coughing my heart up. Aunt

Tina insisted I see a doctor but I never go to a doctor if I didn't really need to. I knew it was just a cold and it would go away eventually. Even though it lasted longer than it normally did, it finally went away but came back a little bit before I headed to Orlando. My doctor was a guy that I ended up hating anyway. He was a very handsome single man and thought he was better than everybody. All the women went crazy over him, and I just couldn't stand the competition. Once I got settled in Orlando then I planned on finding a better doctor, a woman of course.

"I'm fine man, my nose still runs occasionally but that's just an after effect. What's Aunt Tina up to?"

"I haven't talked to her. How 'bout somebody tried to break into my car the other day. I went in the store to pick up some whip cream and some cherries and I heard my alarm going off. I ran out that store so darn fast and I saw some guy running down the street. I started to get in my car and go after him and beat his ass like he stole something but it wasn't worth it. There was something stuck in my door where the key goes, thank God it didn't break off."

"Whip cream man?" I inquired.

"Is that all you heard? Yeah, whip cream. I had some things to take care of and that's all you need to know."

"Well, I don't go all out like that man. Just show me a bed and I'll be good to go."

"Well, you aren't involved with anyone either. You're twenty-eight years old Tony, when are you going to get a real girlfriend? Every time you claim some woman is your girlfriend, you end up cheating on her with someone else and get caught. This has been going on since you were eighteen man, what's up with that?"

"Don't hate on me Ray, you know there are too many women out there for me to claim just one. I was faithful to Earlene in high school and look where it got me! A broken heart, that's where! Never again! But check this, most women I sleep with are married, so that says what? Sounds like to me that I'm not the only one cheating, now am I? Women are a bunch of gold digging, cheating, and devious hoochies."

Earlene Thomas broke my heart. I was only eighteen but she was the only woman I ever loved. I met Earlene when I was seventeen. I was just starting my 12th grade year when I saw her walk in my classroom. I nearly dated all the fine girls in school but Earlene was new to our school and she was first on my list. After class I stopped her, introduced myself and offered to take her out that weekend. She accepted and seemed to be very interested in what I had to say and gave me her number. Earlene had long brown hair and was very tall. She had the body of a goddess with her perfect sized breasts, long slender legs and a perfectly round butt. All the guys were trying to figure out ways to get in good with her but I beat them all to the punch.

I called her that same night and we talked for hours. She told me how lonely she was since she broke up with her boyfriend Kevin. Kevin was very abusive toward her and cheated on her quite often. She told me how she dumped him and would never even consider getting back with him. We had some of the same interests especially when it came to poetry. I asked her to read me a poem that night and she read me a poem she wrote to Kevin.

"The name of this poem is called "Gone.""

> For the past year and a half I have stood by your side.
> Many nights while you were asleep, I have sat alone and cried.
> The love that I offered you was that of its own kind.
> I gave you a strong woman built with a strong mind.
> But you were so busy trying to see all that you could see-
> While I witnessed you forget all that you could be.
> I tried to support you in your desperate time to grow.
> But it appears that the streets were all you wanted to know.
> I gave you my love to guide you through.
> I accepted all the dreams you wished to come true.
> I put all my trust in you, gave you all my heart.
> And slowly with time you ripped it apart.
> You have given someone else what was sacred to me,
> You loved me so much that you gave her your body.
> And even still I tried to make it through
> But your love for me wasn't as strong as my love for you.
> From the beginning, I have been true to you,

And for the times we shared, most of it was me being blue.
I had once dreamed of the future we had planned,
But you aren't the same way you were when we first began.
And now I must end the relationship that I have built.
You should be filled with regret, smothered in guilt.
But in your eyes, you have done nothing wrong.
And with my eyes open, I now see you gone.
This relationship is over and I must move on.
You had the best woman and now she is gone!!!"

I sat there startled by her words. No one I knew could write like that. It was so emotional. She went on to tell me that she thought I was the finest boy in school and she was so happy I approached her. That weekend we went to the drive-in movie theater. Usually I would be all over her but I actually enjoyed talking to her. I listened to her every word as she turned me on more and more. We spent the whole night talking and laughing, something I've never experienced. I took her home and nervously walked her to her door. I told her what a great time I had and leaned in to give her the most sensuous kiss I've ever given. For the next six months we spent every moment together. Even when we were intimate I felt like we were making love instead of just having sex.

One day I had football practice and she came up to me.

"Tony, I have to cancel our date tonight. Shelly and I are going to study for a test all night because we really want to be prepared."

"Ok, sweetheart I understand. Good luck on your test and call me when you finish studying. I'm just gonna go home after practice. I love you."

"I love you too."

Many girls had told me that. You know when you're young you said that so quickly and it never really meant anything. But this time I meant it. I was falling in love with Earlene Thomas. She meant everything to me. We planned on going to prom together, we planned on going to college together, and we planned on getting married. After practice I went home and waited for my sweetheart to call. When the phone rang I ran to answer it.

"Hello?"

"What's up man? A couple of us are going to Café Deez for some pizza. Are you coming or are you gonna be all up in your girl's face like you've been doing lately?"

Earlene hadn't called. I figured we could go one night without seeing each other so I told John I'd go with him and I met him at Café Deez. When I walked into the café, I saw Shelly and a bunch of girls having pizza at a table by the window. Earlene wasn't with them. When I asked Shelly where she was, she said she hadn't seen her all night and she thought she was with me. When I asked Shelly about the test they had tomorrow she told me there was no test. I sat there the rest of the night wondering why Earlene would lie to me about going to Shelly's house. After we ate our pizza, I rode by her house. When I knocked on the door her mother told me she had gone out with a friend and should be back soon.

I parked on the side of the house and sat in the car and waited. After thirty minutes of listening to a mix rap cassette, I turned on the radio where they played nothing but love songs. I sat up in my seat when I saw a car pulling up in her driveway. Some tall handsome guy got out and went to open the passenger side of the car to let Earlene out. They stood there at the door talking for a minute and then they kissed passionately. My heart broke as I watched my girl kissing some other guy. When the guy drove off and Earlene went inside her house, I pulled off. There was a tear in my eye but I refused to cry. Men didn't cry anyway.

When I got home I picked up the phone to call her but saw that there was a message on my answering machine. When I checked my message it was Earlene. She began telling me what a wonderful six months she'd had but she went out with Kevin tonight. She said Kevin was sorry about the way he treated her and that he wanted to get back together. After she contemplated it several times, she agreed to try again. She told me she loved me and she was sorry. I dropped the phone and couldn't believe what I was hearing. I didn't call her back. I was sick the rest of the night. I couldn't eat, I couldn't sleep, and I didn't go to school that whole week after. She called me several times but I told Uncle Steve to tell her I didn't want to talk to her.

When I got back to school the following week she came up to me and told me she had something to tell me.

"What the hell you got to tell me?" I was angry enough.

"Well, I'm pregnant. I just wanted you to know."

I couldn't believe my ears. *Is it mine?*

"Pregnant? By me?" I asked.

She looked down as she whispered, "No, well, at least I don't think so."

"You don't think so? You don't know? Well, how far along are you, a couple weeks?"

"No, I'm three months." She looked away from me as she spoke.

Three months? I couldn't believe what I was hearing. We had been together for six months and she said she didn't think it was mine. She had been cheating on me all this time. What happened to the "I'm a good woman" speech she repeatedly told me? How could I be so stupid? All those nights she claimed to be at Shelly's, she was with Kevin. And now she's pregnant and doesn't know who the father is. I was speechless.

"Tony, it may be yours but it may not be."

"Please leave me alone! Don't talk to me ever again. Do you understand me? Never! When you have that baby and you find out the baby isn't Kevin's then I will take a blood test and see if the baby is mine. If it's mine, I will take care of mine. Other than that, I don't want anything else to do with you."

She just started to cry and yell out how sorry she was while I walked away from her. She was the first and the last to break my heart. Now I'm the heartbreaker. I never heard from Earlene again so I assumed the baby wasn't mine. She had, by far, been the prettiest woman I'd ever been with but I would never forget the nights I laid awake after we broke up. I lost ten pounds because I couldn't eat and I couldn't stand to see her. That was the day I decided I wasn't going to invest any of my time in another woman because they're just not worth it. I heard Ray yelling in the phone bringing me back to reality.

"Tony, hello?"

"Ray, don't talk to me about things that happened to me in my past. I'm not worried about any of these women out here, I'm trying to handle my business and I'll let you handle your business. I have to finish unpacking and you should be here helping me but I have to come back to Miami tomorrow to take care of some unfinished business. I don't start work till another two weeks and I think I'll chill up there for about a week before I come back to this lonely place. I'll hit you up when I get there, peace."

I looked at all the empty boxes everywhere and decided to wait till later to throw them out. I sat on my bed and thought about all the women I've been with. Sometimes it felt like I was the luckiest man in the world to get any woman I wanted, but other times when I walked away from a woman I slept with, I would sit down and have a drink and find myself getting depressed. Sometimes I wished I had the courage and the strength to commit to one woman but the truth of the matter was I was just afraid. It's hard to admit it to myself and I would never admit it to anyone else. I'd ran across those liberal women who tried to tell me why I was such a dog but I argued them down till they just ended up giving up but deep inside I knew they were right. I just couldn't imagine giving some beautiful woman my heart, giving her my all and even marrying her and then to know that one day it would all be over. One day I would lose her over some foolishness or over some temptation one of us couldn't resist. To think that one day we could spend days and even nights arguing about the smallest things. One day the love we had for each other would be gone, that we would one day get tired of seeing each other, and even tired of hearing the other person's voice. I didn't know if my heart could handle such a loss and I just didn't feel I'd met anyone that I was even willing to give a chance.

I fixed me a glass of Hennessey and stared out the window, only time would tell my future. I spent the entire morning hanging up all the clothes I brought down with me. As soon as I was done I took all of the unpacked boxes to the dumpster and headed back to Miami. I went straight to Aunt Tina's house and crashed on the couch. The plan was to take my things to Orlando and spend the entire two weeks there, fixing up my place and enjoying my time alone before I started my new job. But that didn't happen. I really didn't like being alone and being in a place where I knew no one. I was going to try to convince Ray to move back with me, but that probably wouldn't happen either. For that following week, I spent all my time with my brother since his girlfriend was out of town. We spent just about every night shooting pool, getting drunk and talking junk. I didn't try to pick up any women while I was there because I just wanted to enjoy my time with my brother. Ray and I talked about the old times and how we used to dream of becoming police officers when we were younger. That dream quickly changed when a friend of ours was killed by a police officer when he was outside playing with a fake gun. They thought it was real and shot him to death; he was twelve years old.

By the end of the week I tried really hard to convince Ray to move to Orlando with me right before I headed back to my new home.

"Man, you know it'll be the right thing to do. I need my brother and my best friend there with me."

"Tony, you know I can't leave my job. I just got promoted to head journalist." Ray was a journalist for the leading newspaper in Miami. He started there as a clerk when he first finished college and worked his way up to head journalist. He was the most sought after journalist in Florida and I often felt a slight jealousy develop when I thought about the level of his success. After he went into details about his new position, I gave up on the idea of having my brother in Orlando with me. The good thing about it was that Orlando was only a few hours away, so he was still very close. He promised to come visit me once I got settled in and I found myself looking forward to it.

I got back to my new home that Tuesday night and spent the rest of the week indoors arranging everything in my new place. It felt good to lay on the couch in peace and quiet. My body felt exhausted so I got caught up on some much needed rest. I was a little nervous about starting my new job Monday morning but I knew it would be the start of a fast growing career. I heard they did a lot of promoting within the Corporate Office and I had the attitude and charm to get to the very top within a short period of time. They felt that if you were qualified enough to relocate to their office, then you were an asset to the company and they did their best to keep you. I felt fortunate enough to even get a chance to be a part of the Corporate Office, so I vowed to give my all. I was ready for what my new life had to offer.

Chapter Four

RAVEN: THE GIFT

The home phone woke me from my sleep.

"Hello?"

"Hey baby, whatcha doing?

I sat up quickly when I realized it was Terrance. I looked at the time- 4:13 A.M.

"Baby, are you ok?" I asked.

"I'm fine, hung out with the fellas and fell asleep. I'm on my way home now."

"Who are you with Terrance? I've been calling you all darn day! You couldn't call me back earlier?"

"Look baby, I told you I was…" and then I heard a dial tone.

"Hello?" I was so furious that I called Shyla to tell her about what just happened.

"Girl, he screwing someone else, why else would he not call you? And he hasn't even called you back when the phone got disconnected. He ain't fooling nobody!" Shyla thought she was a great renowned psychic when it came to men. She knew when they lied, when they cheated, and how to play their games better than they did.

"If I told you once, I've told you a thousand times, everybody cheats. Go out and find someone to give it to you good and you will feel a lot better! You won't be sitting around crying and calling me at 4 in the morning, instead you'll be getting your freak on. Forget Terrance! If that dog wanna stay out all night then two can play that game. You got to play hard ball girl, you hear me girl? Hello?"

I sat in amazement listening to her. *What kind of advice was that?* This is a time for comforting and she's telling me to do the very thing I didn't want him doing. Terrance was the only man I'd been with since I first laid eyes on him. I couldn't even imagine myself kissing another man. The thought was absurd and I couldn't forgive Shyla for even suggesting such a thing. I wished I had a sister in Christ to call on in my time of need but I hadn't found any female friends in my church as of yet. There was this one girl named Kathy that I seemed to connect with but I didn't want to call her at this time of night.

"I hear ya Shyla, but I'm gonna go ahead and get off the phone now, thanks."

"Girl, think about what I said, I'll call you back later, bye."

I just sat there in the same corner I fell asleep in, listening to the dial tone. I felt tears running down my face. Just the thought of Terrance kissing and making love to someone else ripped me apart. 4:45 A.M. He didn't even call me back. I had to get to work in a few hours and I knew I'd be exhausted once I got there. I felt myself dozing off again.

'BBRRINGG'- My alarm startled me. 6:40 A.M. Terrance was still not home yet nor did he call. I felt anger all throughout my body, *what excuse did he have for this one?* I made up my mind he wouldn't gonna get away with this one regardless of what he said. I got up and searched through my closet, *what am I gonna wear today?* It was a choice between my purple suit or my green one. I chose the green one, laid it out on my bed, said a prayer and jumped in the shower.

"Baby, I'm home."

I turned off the shower, did I hear right? Was it Terrance? I got out, dried myself off and rushed out of the bathroom in a rage. *Who does he think I am?* I walked into my bedroom and saw a big box wrapped in gold wrapping paper sitting on our bed. I looked at it in suspense. On top of the box was a card that read: *I don't even want to argue, I just want to take you out to dinner tonight.* I opened the box in excitement, there it was! The prettiest black evening gown I'd ever seen. It was strapless with a split on both sides and was outlined with diamonds. I smiled and ran through the house looking for Terrance.

"Honey, where are you? Terrance, where are you?" I looked out the window and there he was sitting in his car smiling. I opened the front door and yelled.

"Where are you going Terrance? We need to talk."

"You know I have to get to work by 8:00 A.M., I'll talk to you tonight at dinner. Be ready at 6:30 P.M., I love you."

Before I could say anything he had already rolled the window up and started to drive off. I just stood there watching him drive away. Somehow the anger I once felt ceased and I was suddenly excited about wearing my new gown and going to dinner with the man I loved. I closed the door and rushed in the bedroom to get dressed, singing and dancing to Jesus Loves Me. After I was dressed I stopped, looked in the mirror and thought *I knew Terrance loved me!*

When I got to work I was exhausted. I sat in my cubicle and stared at the computer for a couple seconds before I managed to sign on. I worked at Front Mortgage Company, one of the biggest mortgage companies in Orlando. I swore sometimes I dreaded coming to this place. It was a great place to work but there were just too many women there. There were too many attitudes and hormones to have a healthy work environment. Whenever a man was hired, these women acted like they'd never seen a man before. It started feeling like a contest of who's gonna get the man first, regardless if the woman was married or if the man they were after was married, it didn't matter. And gossip was another pain point at that place. Sometimes I just wanted to scream every time I heard a rumor about someone.

Well, other than that it wasn't that bad. They paid well and besides the random hoochies you ran across, there were actually a few mature and well-mannered women working there. Truth be told, a lot of women there didn't like me because they thought I was stuck-up because I kept to myself and did my job. The only person I talked to at work was Shyla. She's in a different department but we always emailed each other and went to lunch together. The women here didn't like me but they actually hated Shyla. She's slept with over half the women's men and plus she was gorgeous. Every time a new male employee was hired, she always had first dibs.

I was a Financial Analyst here and I used to love my job but lately I'd been feeling like I'm stuck in this one position. I researched all the financial inconsistencies with our members and served as a liaison between the members and the bank. It seemed like every time I tried to apply for another position, I'd get a denial letter telling me I wasn't qualified for that particular position. I was ready to make more money and do something different. Terrance brought home a nice paycheck but I wanted to feel a bit more successful and less dependent on him. The thought of Terrance just made me sigh! *Terrance, what am I going to do with Terrance?* I loved him so much but I just didn't know what to do. Sometimes I felt so smothered by him and wanted him to give me some space and then there were other times I felt like I'd give anything just to be smothered by him.

When I checked my email, I saw that Shyla had emailed me. She wanted to know what time Terrance got in and when I was going to pack my bags and leave him. I responded.

'Shyla, I just got to work. I am still upset with you about that prank you did last night. I am not leaving my husband. Matter of fact, he is taking me out to dinner tonight and we are going to make up. He came in a little after I got off the phone with you, we're doing fine.'

I wouldn't dare tell Shyla what time he really got home, at least not right now. I always ended up telling her the truth but I just didn't want to hear her preaching to me. I waited for her to email me back but she didn't. About an hour later I emailed her again.

'Shyla, where are you? Why haven't you responded to my email?'

Still no response. Another hour went by and a man came to my desk carrying a vase with beautiful daisies in it and a balloon that said *I love you.* That Terrance! He always knew how to make me smile. I quickly signed the slip and anxiously took out the card. It read:

'Raven, I'm sorry about the joke last night. Please forgive me. You are my best friend and I love you (even if OTHER people don't) –Shyla.'

Oh my! I couldn't believe she did that. I was so moved. She then sent me an email and asked if we could do lunch. She was outrageous sometimes but other times she could be the best friend ever. I really needed that and she always knew how to cheer me up. At lunch we laughed about the crazy girl on her team. Shyla was a manager over the customer service area. She moved up really quickly in the company and rumor had it that she slept her way to the top but I hadn't confirmed that so I wouldn't know. One of the girls on her team actually called Human Resources on her saying that she was showing favoritism toward the white girls on her team. She accused Shyla of being a racist toward her own kind. I knew that accusation was definitely absurd, if nothing else. Shyla is definitely proud of being black and she's always trying to encourage the black women on her team to go to college and do something better with their lives. If anything, I'd say she shows more favoritism toward the blacks than the whites. Shyla claims to treat everyone fairly but we both knew what the real problem was in the situation. The girl who reported her had her man come bring her lunch one day. Her man just about passed out when he saw her sexy manager Shyla. The girl noticed his drool and they proceeded to have a big argument right there. Shyla came up and asked the man to leave and called the girl in her office where she wrote the girl up for unruly behavior in the workplace.

Shyla wasn't a tad bit concerned about the report on her. She has several friends in Human Resources that she told about the incident before the report on her even came about. After a while of talking about the work place and that crazy situation, we headed toward a conversation I dreaded.

"So girl, I know you're lying about what time Terrance got home. Why are you even thinking about going out with him tonight anyway? He doesn't deserve you going out with him."

I knew that was coming.

"Don't you have a modeling gig to go to tonight? Why are you concerned about what I will be doing? You will be working, right?"

"Darn girl, you really trying to avoid telling me what time he got home. Yeah, I just have to go to the studio to take a couple head shots for some new magazine coming out and I'll be done. Girl, do you not know how beautiful you are? Hell, if I were a lesbian I'd get with you in a second. You deserve better, Raven."

Ok, she was starting to trip. I swear that girl says some of the most off-the-wall things and I wondered where the heck it all came from. She's always been opposed to being with another woman so she was by no means a lesbian. However, she would always admit to being a freak.

"Shyla, I want my marriage to work. Terrance used to do so much for me. We used to go for romantic walks all the time and he'd tell me how much he loved me. I always knew where he was and most of the times he was there with me. I've been praying all night for my husband, and I believe in prayer!"

"Prayer is good and all, Raven, but what has Terrance done for you lately?"

"I will go out with him and I will try to make an effort to work this out. Maybe he's going through some things right now. I want to have a long-lasting marriage with open communication."

"Girl, that fool got him another person on the side and you need to do the same thing."

I held my head down when she said those words. They cut like a knife. The thought of Terrance with someone else was something I didn't want to accept. "Raven, girl I'm sorry. I just know what these guys are about nowadays. A good woman gets a man and you think he's a good one. He does all the things he's supposed to and you think you're in heaven. Once you let your guard down, then he goes sniffing around for something new to play with. And then he stops respecting you, he comes in anytime he feels like it, he doesn't compliment you anymore and barely sleep with you. The freakiness y'all had in the past dies and it just becomes straight 'let's get it over with' sex. After a while you won't get it at all because he'll be too worn out from giving it to someone else. Men like that never realize they have a good thing till she's gone and by then it's too late. But I say get even before you leave. Heck, give that man a taste of his own medicine. If he can do it then so can you. If he stays out till 5 in the morning, then the next night you stay out till 5:00 A.M. in the morning. Don't be no fool for no man Raven."

I just sat there and listened to her. A part of me knew she was right about a man who cheats. She's usually always right when it comes to things like that. But the other part of me didn't want to accept the fact that my marriage was just about over, and that my husband no longer respected me. I knew God would work it out, and yet I knew that God didn't respect adultery either. I felt a tear run down my cheek but I wiped it before Shyla would notice.

"Shyla, I've had enough of this conversation and your worldly advice. When you get you a husband then you can tell me how to deal with mine, until then I don't want to hear anymore of this nonsense. I really want you to go to church with me. It's obvious you don't know God because it's reflecting in your conversation. God believes in marriages and so do I. Do you know how wonderful He is? God is an awesome God and he can change evil into good. He can make light of a heavy situation. He has his hand on me and I believe that my mission in this marriage is to bring my husband to the Lord. And that's exactly what I'm going to do."

I always knew talking about God would get her to become quiet and leave me alone with her foolishness. She sat there staring at me and then just shook her head.

"I'm sure God's not telling you to be a fool for a man but fine! Be an idiot if you want to. Let's get back to work."

The ride back to the job was very tense. No one said anything. Shyla turned the radio up sky-high and drove like a maniac. I am terrified of crazy drivers and she knows that. I just held on for dear life and anticipated getting out of her car. I really wasn't worried about our friendship because we went through this time and time again. She would get mad at me or vice versa and we would go a day or two without speaking to each other and one of us always ended up breaking down and apologizing. Right now I was feeling it would be her doing the apologies.

When I got back to the office I put my head down on my desk. *What am I doing here? This place isn't where I want to be. I should be the executive of a big company or on my way there.* This position I had was a dead-end job and there was no moving up out of it unless I actually went outside this company. Frustrated with my personal life and my work life, I decided to pull up my resume on the computer and make some adjustments to it; it was time to start searching. I would love to come into a different job as a manager or some other position just to embrace a change. I was a bird and I had dreams and this place just wouldn't allow me to fly.

On my way home I stopped at the grocery store to grab a paper. All the good jobs always posted positions in the classifieds. As I stood in line, I noticed the girl standing in the line across from me. She had bright red hair twisted up into a pretty updo and two gold teeth in her mouth, right in the front. She was wearing a tight low-cut shirt that had 'bling bling' on the front of it and some tight red shorts with her butt cheeks hanging out. She flirted heavily with the guy at the cash register and I noticed he didn't ring up all her items. She smiled as he gave her certain items for free. I couldn't help but stare at her. *How could anyone who carried on in that way have any kind of respect for themselves?* All the guys were checking her out and she was grinning from ear to ear. Those are the type of women who would sleep with your man and not care a thing about you or your feelings. Those types usually sat back and collected welfare checks while your man is laid up with them and you are at your job working hard. I felt myself getting angrier and angrier just watching all the men whoop and holla over her. One guy even rubbed her butt and she just smiled and said in a non-convincing way "stop boy!" I know I shouldn't stereotype, Lord forgive me, but it bothers me because of the hard times me and my husband are having right now. I walked out to my car with my paper under my arm and just kept picturing Terrance being one of those guys all over this girl, and in the grocery store of all places! When she walked out the store I couldn't help but walk up to her.

"Excuse me, excuse me. Have I seen you somewhere before?" I knew I didn't know the girl but I was just so curious to see if my presumptions were right about her. I wanted to know where she worked and what side of town she lived on. I assumed she worked at McDonald's or some low paying job that could care less about the things she wore if she even worked at all. My insecurities kicked in and I knew this was something God was working on when it came to my salvation.

"No, I don't think so. Do I look familiar?" she looked at me in curiosity.

"Um, I'm not sure but maybe I can figure it out. Where do you work?"

"I own my own club downtown. Perhaps you've heard of it, it's called The Wordz. I figured you didn't know me from there because I am usually never there or when I am there I'm always in my office in the back taking care of business but it is possible you've seen me there before."

What? I couldn't believe my ears! This girl owned the place I loved to go to, she owned my relaxing getaway spot. I stood there in disbelief. She couldn't have been more than twenty years old, perhaps someone left it to her or maybe she was lying, in fact she must've been lying. Someone who looked that way couldn't own their own business. So I cleared my throat.

"Well, I love that place. I'm there all the time, maybe I have seen you there before. You look a little young to own that place, how did you run across something like that?" I waited impatiently for her response.

"Well, thank you. I've been told I look young a lot. In fact, I love to dress like I'm young as well. Makes me feel so alive, besides, I own a place where people come to express themselves and aren't afraid to say what they feel, wear what they want, and be who they please. But I am thirty-five

42

and I got my Bachelor's degree in business management and invested in my own club. I've always loved poetry and there were never any real poetry clubs out there so I decided to start my own. Well, I've got to be going because my husband's waiting for me. Here's my card."

"Oh, uh okay thank you. My name is Raven."

"Great to meet you, Raven, I'll see you soon." She left me standing there in the parking lot; I couldn't believe how wrong I had been. I guess it's true when they say you can't judge a book by its cover and I felt ashamed that I had. She was right! *The Wordz* is a place that encourages freedom of speech and dress, although I always dressed like a lady. I was wrong to assume she was an uneducated, underpaid hoochie. I looked down at the card she handed me and shook my head when I read *Shayquan Johnson – CEO of The Wordz Poetry Club*, how could I be so shallow? It just made me realize that I really needed to find a new job!

As soon as I got home I took my newspaper and headed straight to the bed. So many jobs were hiring. Oooh here's one: dancers wanted – make up to $1000.00 a night. Yeah right, me a dancer? I think not! I don't care how much they made, nothing would make me degrade myself like that. Besides, I was a new born child of God now. There were tons of medical jobs out there. Hmmm maybe I should've gone to medical school. *Shoot, nothing I qualify for.* Just when I was about to give up, there it was! The ad took up half the page. It was a position at Whitters Insurance Companies of Orlando. They were hiring for a trainer position and I have always wanted to be a trainer. I had plenty of experience training the new employees in my department at Front Mortgage and I inquired several times about their trainer positions but there were never any available. I could work my way up from trainer to manager. I could see it now: Raven Sinclair, manager of the training department. There were four positions available so I had a great chance of getting this job. I jumped on my computer and sent them a copy of my resume. *Look out dreams – here I come!*

Chapter Five

TONY: NOT ON THE FIRST DATE

Look at this place! It's about ten times larger than the insurance company I came from in Miami. I stood there watching all the busy claims and customer service reps.

"Excuse me, you must be Anthony Wilkerson."

I turned around and saw the most beautiful black woman I've seen in Orlando thus far. She had a short haircut, light brown eyes and the black skirt she wore showed off her long lean legs. I'm a sucka for nice legs. Her scent reminded me of a woman I met at the *Lighthouse Club* a couple months ago. It was a sweet vanilla smell that made me tingle.

"Please call me Tony. You must be Sheena."

"No, sorry to disappoint you, I'm Reigene. I will take you to Sheena shortly. I just wanted to meet the new manager. No one told me how handsome you were."

I felt myself blushing.

"Thank you, are there a lot of beautiful women here or are you the only one?"

She smiled, "I think I'm the only one, follow me."

I checked out her shape as we walked. It was something worth grabbing. I couldn't help but picture myself kissing her relentlessly.

"Tony, Sheena's in there waiting for you and please don't hesitate to call me if you ever need someone to take you around town, here's my number."

"Most definitely, thank you." I walked into the room where a huge heavyset woman, black as tar, greeted me. Her hair had lost its curls and her glasses were a bit thick. She smiled showing off the gap between her two front teeth as I cringed at her sight. I suppose Reigene was right, she was the only beautiful one so far.

"Good morning ma'am, I'm Tony Wilkerson, eager to work."

The day seemed to go quickly as Sheena showed me all the ins and outs and the dos and don'ts. I met a couple employees under my supervision and I especially liked Michael. Michael was a black twenty-one year old college student majoring in accounting. He had that same ambition in his eyes as I did when I was his age. Janet, a nineteen year old, was extremely jolly. She had blonde hair and wore a thin style of glasses. One might call her dingy or hyper, but she was known to keep you laughing. Janet talked my head off for a good fifteen minutes about how she loved to swim before Reigene came to save me.

"I got that package you wanted sir, please follow me, excuse us Janet." I walked away quickly.

"Just thought I'd save you, she could talk your ear off for hours if you let her," I gave a sigh of relief.

"Thanks, what are you doing tonight?" I asked. She smiled the prettiest smile. I knew it was against policy to date employees but who cared about policies? Rules were meant to be broken.

"Whatever you want me to do," she said. *Uh, I could think of some things.*

"Well, I wanted to see Orlando and I have no idea where to start."

"Call me and I'll show you everything Orlando has to offer."

I grabbed some paper and wrote down my number for her to have. She tucked the number in her purse and gave me a wink. I watched her walk away as I thought *I'm going to like this place.*

As I walked through my department, I noticed all the cubicles were decorated in different forms that described the person's personality. One girl had pictures of cats plastered all over her cube. There were pictures of stars, family members, cartoon characters and little toys throughout the different cubes. Heck, my cubicle only had insurance documents plastered everywhere when I was in Miami. I had only one picture of myself in a frame on my desk.

"Are you the new assistant manager?"

I turned around to see a tall black man with a thin set of glasses on. He was wearing a tight blue suit with a red and white bow tie. *What day and age was he stuck in?* The man's hair looked as if it hadn't been cut in months and his shiny shoes had somehow lost their shine. Trying my best not to laugh, I reached out my hand to him.

"Yes, I am. And who might you be?"

"I'm Herman. I'm in your department. Have they told you that the manager is out for the remainder of the year? She is out on medical leave. You did know that didn't you?"

"Of course I knew that. What exactly is it you do, are you on the phones?" I asked.

"Yes sir, I am. We are half inventory and half customer service. I am the person they come to for assistance."

"Well Herman, I will be holding a meeting in a little while to meet the rest of the employees in my department. Please tell everyone to come to the area behind my office at 2:05 P.M."

"Of course, sir."

"Please, call me Tony."

I walked into my cubicle that they called an office. It was the biggest cubicle in the department. *Man, I wish I had windows in here.* I couldn't complain though, I was definitely making more money and earning more respect. I looked at the time; 1:58 P.M. Well, I had a couple more minutes to relax before I got a chance to find out who I'd be managing. I sat out the picture of myself and placed it on my desk. I loved this picture. Ray took this picture of me when I won first place in the statewide poetry contest. It was a very happy day for me. I was twenty-two years old and dreamed of writing a poetry book one day. I've always wanted to serenade the women with my romantic words but reality took its hold over me and I never got a chance to even start on a poetry book. The closest I come to it now was when I wrote my poems in my notebook from time-to-time.

One by one I noticed people walking behind my office. It was documented to be twenty workers under my supervision. I waited till Herman came to the office to tell me they were all waiting before I made my entrance. All the women employees blushed as I introduced myself.

"Hello, my name is Anthony Wilkerson, your new assistant manager. I would like everyone to please call me Tony. Let me tell you a little about myself. I'm from Miami and I'm new to this city. I'm twenty-eight years old and I'm single with no kids. I worked for Whitters Insurance Companies

46

of Miami as a Quality Coach in the claims department. I worked hard throughout all the years that I was there and tried to learn all that I could so I could be where I am now. I don't believe in micro-managing, therefore I would like to think everyone would do their jobs and be on their best behavior. I believe in having fun also so we will occasionally plan fun things to do as a team. In my spare time, I enjoy working out and writing poetry. Now that you know a little about me, I want to go around the room and have everyone introduce yourself and tell me a little bit about yourself."

Each person spoke briefly about him or herself and welcomed me to the department. For the most part I was pleased with my team members. Herman seemed to be the most knowledgeable about the position and I already knew he would make my job a lot easier. There was this beautiful Indian woman on our team as well. Her name was Guitree and she was thick in all the right places. When she spoke, she made sure she mentioned the fact that she was single and looking. She was thirty-two and had one daughter. I made a mental note and waited for Reigene to speak.

"My name is Reigene. I'm twenty-five and I'm single. I live with a roommate and my pastime is reading. I'm in college right now part-time majoring in photography. I've been with the company for three years and I look forward to working with you."

She winked at me when she was finished and I tried to hide the smile that was trying to escape from my mouth. Once everyone was done, I opened the floor up for questions, concerns or comments. No one had anything to say and before we knew it, the meeting was done. For the rest of the day I arranged my cubicle and refreshed my knowledge on the inventory procedures and noted any differences from our techniques in Miami. Right in the middle of reviewing my papers, Sheena walked up with a tall white man with dark curly hair. When I stood up to greet them, Sheena introduced him as the Director of the department. He shook my hand and blushed the way the women would when they met me. If I didn't know any better I would've sworn he was checking me out. Only when he spoke did I know my suspicions were correct.

"I'm David Patten. It is a pleasure to finally meet you. I've heard so much about you Tony. If you have any problems of any sort then please don't hesitate to stop by my office upstairs."

He grinned from ear to ear. It was obvious this man had more sugar in him than a sweet potato pie.

"Thank you, sir. Hopefully I won't have any problems. I'm just organizing right now and trying to get situated."

"Well, I would like to hold a meeting with you this week or next week to go over my expectations. You were hired as the assistant manager, however, in the next couple months we may end up making you the manager according to your job performance and the status of the previous manager. I will be getting in touch soon, have a great day."

Manager? Hmmm, I liked the way that sounded. More money would definitely come with that. I'm the acting manager anyway now that the previous manager is out. Things are really starting to come together and suddenly I wished Ray could enjoy it with me. Ray was my only immediate family and I love him more than any brother could. I figured if I played my cards right, within the next three to four years I could be Director. Heck, all I had to do was flirt with David hard enough. Now, I didn't get down with men, even though once I was really attracted to one. I know that if I were drunk enough I would've fallen in that trap. Thank goodness I wasn't *that* drunk.

His name was Tiki. I was at the *Lighthouse Club* in Miami on poetry night and in walked this man. He was light-skinned and had long hair that was braided in a zigzag style. His smile was perfect; super straight teeth and pretty lips. I must admit at first I wasn't attracted to him because I had never in my life been attracted to a man. After a while, I started thinking how nice looking he was and how it didn't make me jealous that all the women had their eyes glued to him. In most cases like this I would feel envious of the man but for some reason I didn't feel that way with Tiki; he had my attention as well. He looked like a thugged-out Prince with these big light brown eyes. After a couple drinks, I found myself staring at him and ignoring the beautiful woman sitting at my table. When he got up to read his poem, I found myself glued to his every word. This was scaring me. I'd never felt like this before.

"Hello, my name is Tiki. This is my first time here so I'm a little nervous. Bear with me y'all. The name of this piece is *Why.*"

I waited anxiously to hear the words that would come out his mouth.

"You look at me, beautiful you think, you think beauty. All you can see are these beautiful eyes surrounded by light caramel skin and mother Africa's full lips and you see beauty. I've struggled. Struggled through hard times, fought to have more than I was given. Destined to fail, determined to win. Living life the way I am, I was faced with society's rules and regulations. The odds were against me. All you see is beauty. I screamed in my fears, fears of no way out this secluded life. This society life I was born – into a world with no understanding, no easy way out. Associated with stereotypes- young black gay man, faggot, homo, fruitcake, a disgrace, and an outcast. So, I graduate with diploma in left hand and pride in the right. Pretending to be what society would call normal. I dated women and smiled in my parent's faces with painful delight. I wallowed in my sorrow, afraid to be who I am, afraid to be the person I was born to be and yet, when you look at me you see nothing but this beauty. Now here I am with pride in my left hand and pride in my right as I stand up and say I'm proud to be who I am. I am proud to be who I was destined to be. Now, when some look at me they don't see such beauty because they feel I've disgraced them. My beauty can't define the shame they feel. But now when I look in the mirror I see beauty, a kind of beauty I've never noticed before. Why can't you see what I see? Why?"

The audience was quiet for a second or two. The women were trying to grasp the fact that this was a fine gay man standing in front of them and the words he spoke were so deeply recited that some even had tears in their eyes. Before I knew it, half the audience was on their feet whooping and hollering. I sat there all of a sudden wanting to hear more, to see more, and to my surprise, to know more. When Tiki sat down, I walked over to him to tell him how great I thought his poem was but before I could get the words out, he cut me off.

"I have been watching you watching me all night. What's your name?"

"Tony. My name is Tony." Ok, now I felt like I was tripping for real because I told this man my real name. I was confused about what was happening here. Not once in my life had I ever even thought about another man.

"Tony, please join me for a drink."

I looked around. All these women in here knew my face and I didn't want any of them getting the wrong idea about me.

"How 'bout we get out of here and go somewhere else to drink. Maybe down the street to *The Rage*. What do you say?" I asked.

He finished his drink in one gulp and told the woman he came with that he would be back later and looked at me with a smile on his face. I didn't want anyone to see me walk out with him so I told him I had to make a stop somewhere and would meet him there in about fifteen minutes. On my ride down the street, I suddenly became nervous. I've never been to *The Rage* but I heard it was a gay club. I figured if anyone saw me in there then they would be gay anyway and I wouldn't care. We spent the whole night talking and drinking. He was really aggressive with his words and I felt so uncomfortable. I told him this was all new to me and about my whole unexplained attraction to him. But deep in my heart I knew it was nothing but the devil.

"Would you like to go back to my place? I won't bite. We can just hang out and maybe watch a movie or something," he inquired.

I agreed. When we walked into his apartment I noticed how small it was. There was a black futon disguised as a couch in the living room and a stand with a thirteen inch color television on it with a VCR sitting unstably on top of it. The kitchen was extremely small and a pile of dirty dishes was lying in the sink. We sat on the futon and smiled at each other. I kept thinking I must have lost my head for even being here. I truly love women so I just felt extremely confused.

"Are you going to turn on the TV?" I asked nervously.

"I'd rather turn you on." Tiki reached over and kissed me softly on the lips. It was a little peck but I freaked out and jumped up as fast as I could.

"Tiki, I can't do this." He looked irritated yet understanding, if that was possible. He laid back on the futon and just stared at me while I paced the living room floor back and forth.

"I'm sorry, I didn't mean to mislead you. I am not gay. I am very attracted to you for some odd reason and I had a great time talking to you and getting to know you. Please don't be angry with me."

Tiki just sat there for a second and then he dropped his head in his hands.

"Tony, it's ok. I understand. I was just really hoping we would hit it off. Please keep my number, just in case."

I took the long way home that night trying to comprehend what just happened and I was shaken at what could've happened. I didn't pray often but I thanked God for saving me from destruction. I knew I wasn't living right with all the women in and out my life, but this would've been even worse and my family would never understand. The devil almost got me good.

That was the only guy I had ever been attracted to and there were none after that. This David Patten Director guy was definitely no looker, anyway. I figured I would have an advantage over my position at work because I knew he thought I was fine but then again, who didn't?

I left work around 3:45 P.M. and stopped at the Fun House for a slice of pizza. The Fun House was directly across the street from a college and seemed to be the hangout spot for all the students. As I sat down to enjoy my food and relax, I read the paper and watched all the college students walk past the window.

"Are you here all by yourself?" I looked up to see a skinny white girl with long red hair, blue eyes and a pretty smile.

"Unfortunately, I am. Care to join me?" She sat down.

"I'm Wendy. I'm a student at the college across the street. Do you go there?" I noticed the clothes she had on. Her red blouse didn't seem to be large enough to cover her breasts because they were practically hanging out. She had on some very tight black leather pants, which made her butt look flatter than it actually was.

"I'm new in town, my name is Randy. I'm visiting my sick mother and I've been kinda lonely, you know a man has needs." I could tell from her clothes and the smile she gave me after that statement that she would be an easy lay.

"Well, how about I show you around the school and the dorms where I live?" I had another slice of pizza left so I invited her to hang out with me until I was done. I sat there and listened to her blab on and on about the diversity of students at her school and how skilled her teachers were. She was from Delaware and wanted to major in art but since her parents were paying for her education they wanted her to major in law. She took pride in her school and gave anyone she met a tour in hopes that they would want to be a part of the school as well. When we were ready for the tour of the school, she took me directly to the dorms next door to the Fun House.

"I have to get something out of my room really quick, come on in," I came in and looked around the small room. On her wall were pictures of Madonna, unlike her roommate's pictures who plastered her wall with Malcolm X and Martin Luther King, Jr. Wendy had vanished into her bathroom while I checked out the daisies outside her window. They were shaped in a circle and blossomed so freely as the wind blew.

"Are you ready to see the University?" I truly didn't want to see the school she bragged so much about.

"Why don't we sit here and get to know each other a little better before you give me the tour." She hesitated for a second, checked her watch and let out a big

"Sure OK!"

I found myself wishing I were one of the daisies outside as I sat on the edge of the bed and Wendy nearly talked my ear off. I had zoned her out for the past five minutes.

"Randy, well?" I looked at the hyper girl next to me in confusion. What in the world was she talking about?

"Uh, well what?" I inquired.

"Don't you agree?"

"Of course I agree." I had no idea what I said I agreed to, and I didn't much care either. Wendy started to open her mouth to talk again and I quickly put my fingers to her lips, *thank goodness!*

"Don't talk! Those lips are too sweet for another word. I'll die if I can't kiss them." The smile that followed my words made Wendy's face look like the Joker. I kissed her first on the cheek, next on the lips and then on the neck. I felt her tremble as I started to unbutton her blouse. *This is extremely too easy*, I thought. The first thing Wendy did was drop to her knees. After only a couple minutes I felt a sigh of relief and Wendy went to the bathroom to freshen up. My main concern was getting pleasure for myself and since I did, I was ready to leave.

"Are you ready for the main course?" She walked out completely naked.

"Hun, I have got to get going, I'm sorry," she looked at me in disgust as I buckled my belt.

"What? Why?" she seemed very disappointed.

I wanted to say *I got mine so I'm happy* but instead I just said

"I don't sleep with girls on the first date and if you do, then that only means one thing – that you're a slut. I can't respect a girl like that. Goodbye." As I closed the door behind me I heard her scream "you jerk!"

Chapter Six

RAVEN: THE RENEWAL

"This place is beautiful Terrance, where did you find it?" 16th Street Tunes was a classy jazz restaurant. The place was crowded with laid back folks as I sat and admired my husband. He was wearing a black suit with a black and brown satin tie. The diamond in his ear shone brighter than it ever had. He was looking darn good.

"Raven, I know I haven't been the man you want me to be but I promise I'll try. I got caught up with my boys last night. There is no excuse and I don't even wish to talk about it right now, it just makes me angry thinking about their foolishness. I want to apologize to you and I've been thinking about renewing our marriage vows and starting over fresh. I struggled with the idea all night and I didn't want to face you until I decided what I wanted to do. So, do you think you would do me the honor of becoming my wife, again?"

I felt tears run down my face. God does answer prayers.

"Yes, of course. This is the best night I've had in a long time."

"Well, I'm glad to hear that. I hope we have many more."

"Can I ask you one thing Terrance? Why don't you return my calls when I call you? If we are married, we should be able to trust each other and I must admit I don't really trust you much right now. I've been praying and-" he cut me off.

"You don't trust me? How could you even say a thing like that? What do you want me to do, check in with you twenty-four hours a day? Darn, a brotha can't take a dump without having to call you and tell you about it, is that it? You want me to tell you my every move? I'm sick of this! I tried to make tonight special for you but you got to ruin that too. If anything, I shouldn't trust you. You and Shyla go to y'all little poetry readings every Thursday night, or so you say. How do I know you and Shyla not creeping? Besides, I never liked that Shyla anyway, she's a hoe and you know she is. You running around here talking about you're saved and all holy, so why are you hanging out with someone like her? Can you tell me that?"

"Terrance, calm down. How could you even fix your mouth to say I'm cheating on you? Terrance, I'm home every night. I love you Terrance. And Shyla is a good person and she's not a hoe. She was there for me when no one else was. But she has nothing to do with us. I love you." Tears rolled down my cheek.

"Well, act like it. Waiter!" he called the waiter over and ordered for the both of us. He didn't even ask me what I wanted, he just ordered me a salad.

"I don't see how you can even say you wanted to be a model, you need to lose weight. How much do you weigh now?" he questioned.

"Being 5'6"and 145 pounds is the perfect weight and I am not into that modeling thing anymore, you'd know that if you were around more."

"Well, you need to start working out. I like women Shyla's size."

I couldn't believe where this conversation was going. How did we go from exchanging wedding vows to I need to lose weight? I got plenty modeling deals when I was modeling but I decided modeling just wasn't for me. I didn't say another word after that sly comment about comparing me to Shyla, I couldn't believe he went there. He continued to go on and on about how he is faithful and he don't know why I'm so paranoid and how I'm being too possessive over him. I just ate my salad and didn't say a word.

"What's your problem?" he yelled.

I just looked at him like he was the stupid idiot he was acting like and continued to eat my salad.

"Waiter!" I yelled. I was hungry as heck, and I didn't just want a salad. I was going to order me some real food.

"What are you calling the waiter over for? Hello? Do you hear me talking to you? You're not talking to me, what's wrong?" he said.

"What's wrong? *We* are what's wrong. How can you stay out all night, take me to dinner and discuss renewing our vows and then turn around and insult me?"

Terrance gave me a snobby grin and just as he was about to speak the waiter walked up.

"Yes ma'am, may I help you?"

"Yes sir, I'm done with this salad. I would like to order some real food now. Give me the chicken alfredo pasta dinner with no tomatoes, thank you."

Terrance started to shake his head but I started speaking before he could get any ignorant remarks out.

"Terrance, you are starting to be really annoying. I was so excited about this dinner date even though I should've been furious at you for staying out all night. Am I doing something wrong Terrance? Aren't you in love with me anymore?" I waited anxiously for his answer.

"I love you Raven. You are the only one I want. I'm just stressed out with work and all."

"What's going on at work? I thought y'all hired Sherry to assist you with all the paperwork, isn't that helping?" I asked, knowing that we were changing the subject.

"Yeah, Sherry's great. It's not the paperwork that's stressing me out. We have a new group that is off the chain and we've already gotten several companies looking to sign them. However, the one offering the top amount of money to sign them doesn't want our company to do the production on their album. We tried to go with the second highest offer from a different company but the group is dead set on going with the top one. It seems hard for us to convince them otherwise and I feel like I'm going to lose one of my best groups."

"You did all the music on their first album! You could fight the company if they try not to use you."

"They don't want to use any of the songs we've done on their album, and if they do use a few then they will compensate me for it. It's a bunch of bull."

"Well maybe you should talk to the group more, give them an incentive for staying with your production. You can do it."

"Yeah, perhaps you're right. How are things going at your job?"

"Same ole same ole! I can't move up in the company because they have a hiring freeze right now. I get so frustrated because I'm not where I want to be. I should be a manager by now like Shyla."

"Yeah, Shyla got it going on, brains and beauty." I just looked at him with an *'I wanna slap the taste out your mouth'* look. What's with all this Shyla talk like he's interested in her or wishes he had seen her first that night? Usually Terrance is downing Shyla saying how much of a hoe she is and how he can't believe Justin finally got her to settle down but tonight he was acting like she is just this ideal woman, let him tell it.

"Terrance, when are you going to go to church with me? Pastor said it's good when both parties in the marriage come to God. It would mean a lot to me."

"Pastor said, Pastor said. I'm so tired of hearing about what Pastor said. I'll go with you when you stop telling me everything Pastor said. How 'bout that?"

I couldn't believe how easy it was for him to bring me down.

"I need you to go to church with me."

"Fine, maybe I'll go soon." He changed the subject again and started talking about how he will miss his group if they leave. I just sat there most of the time pretending to listen as I tried to build my mood back up. We finished our food and talked a little about his plans for the company.

"Terrance, let's make tonight the start of something new." I interrupted.

"Ok baby, let's do that! Come on, let's get out of here."

On the way out the restaurant a woman stopped us. She was absolutely beautiful and it looked like she belonged on the cover of a magazine. She had legs to die for and this really short dress that curved her body like a glove. Her hair was cut short in layers and her make-up was almost flawless. She did a double take when she saw us and smiled.

"Hey baby, is this your sister?" *Sister? Am I his sister?!!! What kind of junk is that?* So I politely cut Terrance off and replied.

"No dear, I'm Raven, his wife and you are?"

"His wife?" she said in a shocking voice. Just as I was going to respond, Terrance grabbed my arm, told the lady she must be mistaken and dragged me out of the restaurant.

The drive home was silent. I was fuming by this time… what was going on? Was this someone Terrance was messing around with? Was this a friend or family member of someone Terrance was involved with? I felt tears run down my face.

"Terrance, we need to…" He turned the radio up sky high before I finished. When we got home I stormed out of the car, tears running freely and went straight to the room. Terrance took a while before he got to our room. It sounded like he made a couple of phone calls because I could hear his muffled voice from time to time. After a while I heard him try to turn the knob, but of course I locked him out.

"Raven, open this door – NOW!"

"You sleep on the couch for now on until you're ready to talk about what happened tonight."

"Raven, I want to talk about it now – open the door baby."

I thought about it for a second. I wanted to tell him no but then again I really wanted to hear what he had to say about this. When I opened the door he sat on the bed.

"Baby, let me talk before you say anything. I promise you I have never seen that woman before in my life. I think she thought I was someone else and I didn't have time to entertain fools, that's why I grabbed you and left. I love you and only you, Raven. About renewing our vows, I thought of a day. Hmm… how 'bout next weekend? We can go down to the church tomorrow and set it up. I want you to know how much I love you and that I'm willing to renew our marriage, and I promise I'll start going to church with you too. Baby, I want nothing more right now than to make things right and to make love to you."

I couldn't say a word, what was I to say? He got up from the bed and kissed me gently. He hadn't kissed me that way in a long time. We were up all night making love over and over again, my heart started beating intensely as I felt his every breath on my neck. That was a feeling I had back when we first got married and a feeling I truly missed. God knew I loved that man; I would give him my all!

When I woke up in the morning Terrance had breakfast cooking. I threw on my robe and walked down to the kitchen where he stood butt naked. *Darn he looked good.* Such a fine body and I always loved his perfectly round butt.

"Good Morning, beautiful." He walked over and gave me the sweetest kiss. Wow, I missed this. He used to cook me breakfast all the time when we dated but after we got married it stopped. I always loved Saturdays because that was my day to relax and go shopping but today I just looked forward to spending the day with my husband.

"So, what do you want to do today? I was thinking maybe catch a movie and go out dancing," I inquired.

"Baby, I made plans with Donnie. I thought you and Shyla might be hanging out like you usually do." Donnie was one of his no-good friends from back in the days. I never liked him because he was married and always running around on his wife. His wife Vera knew about it but didn't seem to really care as long as Donnie was paying all the bills and giving her money to go shopping. She's a really big and unattractive lady, so I don't think she's ever cheated on him. Donnie, on the other hand, is a nice looking older man and all the women practically threw themselves at him. When Donnie married Vera, she was only 125 pounds but now she was sneaking right up to 200 pounds. I have always thought a woman should remain fit and looking good for herself and for her husband. However, I still didn't feel like that's an excuse to go out and cheat on her.

"Well, I'm not going out with Shyla tonight because I want to spend time with my husband. Can't you cancel your plans? We've been going through a lot the past couple months and I think we really need to start spending more time together. Besides, you know how I feel about you hanging out with Donnie all the time. Seems like every other night you're over Donnie's house or going out with Donnie. You sure you're not married to him?" I said sarcastically.

"There you go nagging me again. Can't we go a day without arguing? This is why I stay gone all the time because when I'm around, you always find something to argue about. I'm always doing something you don't like and saying something you don't want to hear. Donnie is my friend whether you like him or not. Donnie isn't too fond of you either but you don't hear him telling me to divorce you. I need guy time."

"Jesus, how much guy-time do you need? When will you need wife-time? I'm sick of this Terrance, sick of it! What time are you going out with him?"

"After breakfast I'm taking a shower and heading out to the gym with Donnie. We will be out the rest of the day and probably hitting the clubs tonight. I should be home around 2:00 A.M."

"So you mean to tell me you are going to be gone the whole day and night? Clubs? Here I am trying to live right and my husband is out partying at the clubs!"

"You go to a club every Thursday night, you hypocrite!" he yelled.

"I go to an elegant poetry spot, they don't play all that devil music and they have tables and chairs so everyone is sitting down listening to featured poets. They also have food there, so it's more of a social gathering as opposed to a club. It's nothing like those drug-infested clubs you go to. The only reason people go there is to dance dirty all night to that devil music and to pick up on someone. Which reason are you going for?"

"I am going to socialize with my boy!" he said mockingly.

"What do you take me for Terrance, a fool? Why do you keep taking me on these emotional roller coasters? One day I'm happy with you and the next I'm disgusted with you. I don't deserve this. If you don't want to be married to me anymore then let me know 'cause right now you are living your life as if you're single."

"Look, I want to be married to you but you have got to change your attitude. I want to be able to enjoy my life and I don't need you making me feel guilty every time I want to go out and have a good time."

I stood up and looked him straight in the eyes.

"Are you cheating on me, Terrance?"

"Don't ask me no stupid junk like that," he snarled and walked away. I sat there in disbelief. What just happened? I sat down at the table and cried. At first I wanted to do what Shyla suggested- go out and cheat on him but I couldn't. I wouldn't allow anyone, not even Terrance, to make me backslide. I did know that I didn't want my marriage to end. There had been quite a few gorgeous men trying to holla at me but I always stayed true to Terrance, even in our weakest moments. It seemed like Terrance had lost all respect for me and I didn't know what I'd done to make things this way. He had even called me out of my name a few times and disregarded everything I said as if it went through one ear and out the other. He didn't take me seriously at all anymore. The more I thought about it the angrier I got. I stormed in the bathroom inside of our room where he was getting out of the shower and yelled.

"Terrance, I'm sick of this. You hear me, I'm sick of it. I love you, Terrance. Why are you treating me so cold?" Terrance kept drying himself off as if he didn't even realize I was standing there. He was ignoring me. I ran to the closet in our room and grabbed a hand full of his clothes and threw it at him. That got his attention.

"Get out! I don't want you anymore if you are going to continue to disrespect me the way you do. I want you out my house. Now!" I yelled.

Terrance looked at me in surprise. This was the first time I'd ever told him to get out and I could tell he was starting to get furious. He had this look in his eyes I've never seen before and it made me terrified. Before I knew it he had slapped me so hard I fell to the floor. Terrance had never hit me before. I screamed and jumped back on my feet and he slapped me down again, this time yelling.

"If you ever tell me to leave the house I pay bills in again I will kill you, Raven. You understand? I will kill you. This is *my* house and I'm not going anywhere, you hear me?" I sobbed on the floor as I wiped the blood from my lip.

"Pick my damn clothes up." He grabbed the clothes he laid out to wear and walked out of the room, slamming the door behind him. I just laid on the floor stunned. This was the man I fell in love with. I didn't know what to do. I knew I'd done nothing to deserve this. I come home from work every day and I always had dinner waiting for him. All I asked was that he spent more time with me. All I asked was that he showed me some respect and all I got was this. I sat there sobbing for more than ten minutes until I heard the front door open. I jumped up and ran to the living room but Terrance was already in his car pulling off. I sat on the floor, leaning up against the foot of my bed, and grabbed my journal.

Entry Number 3:

> When I look out my window I picture you in my mind.
> The loving smile upon your face is suddenly so hard to find.
> The delightful glow on your face, the sparkling glisten in your eyes.
> All are so hard to see right now, they are hidden by all your lies.
> They are hidden by your cheating and also by my tears.

They are hidden by all my faith that had suddenly turned
to fears.
When I looked out my window, your face seemed to be
drowned by the rain.
And as soon as the pouring stops, I'll be drowned in all
my pain.
But, I'll never look out my window again unless I see the
morning sun
that gives me hope and lets me know that another day
has just begun
And so can I…

I cleaned myself up and pulled myself together. I tried calling Terrance
but he didn't answer so I hung up and called Shyla.

"Shyla, I really need to hook up with you tonight. Terrance and I got
in a fight and I just really need you right now."

"Well, I promised Justin I would go out with him tonight, Raven.
What were y'all fighting about now?"

"He hit me, Shyla."

"What? He hit you? Oh my God Raven, are you ok?"

"I'm fine. I'm just in disbelief and I feel like I'm going to die. I don't
know what to do, Shyla." I felt tears rolling down my face again.

"Girl, I can't believe he hit you! You have got to leave him, Raven.
Don't worry, I will call Justin and cancel. I'm on my way over there.
Stay put."

Before I could say anything Shyla had hung up. She was really a good
friend even though she wasn't saved. I was amazed that she was willing to
cancel a date with Justin for me. Justin was in love with Shyla. She had
slowed down a little once she realized that Justin was serious about being
with her. I think the only reason Shyla messed around so much was because
she often got her heart broken when she tried to settle down with someone.
She had the attitude that she would treat guys the same way they treated
her and that's exactly what she did. Justin was different though. He was
a lawyer and was very successful in his career as well as his love life. He
had accomplished something I didn't think was possible: he got Shyla to

slow down. For the past six months he had been the only man she's been seeing. They'd known each other for over a year but she was still doing her own thing for the first six months. I really prayed that one day they'd get married.

When Shyla arrived to my house we decided to go out to lunch. As soon as we sat down to eat I started to cry hysterically and told her everything that happened. I even told her about the renewal of vows he pulled on me and how stupid I felt for falling for it. I always said I would never let anyone hit me and put up with it because my mother was beat by my father and I never wanted to live that life. Even though that was the first time Terrance ever struck me, I felt like it might become worse if I stayed. His behavior was getting outrageous and I didn't know how much more of it I could take. I listened to Shyla go on and on about how I should move in with her and take Terrance for all he's got. I needed a breather from her so I told her I had to go home and freshen up and we could go out to the poetry club that night. We usually went on Thursdays but I needed to hear some spoken word to ease my mind.

When I got home I went straight to the bedroom. Lying on the bed was a dozen of roses and a balloon that said "I love you." There was a card attached to the balloon. I shook my head as I sat on the bed and opened the card. It read "Raven, I'm sorry. I will be home early tonight." The nerve of him to think that I would be that easily swayed. I wasn't going to change my plans for him after what he'd done. I stepped over his suits still lying on the floor and went to the living room to relax. I laid down on the couch wondering where it all went. Why was my marriage falling apart? Just as I was searching through the channels the phone rang.

"Hello?"

"Hey Raven, it's me, Kathy. What's going on?"

"Kathy? Hey girl, how did you get my number?"

"Pastor gave it to me because something in my spirit told me to call you. I hope you don't mind."

"No, not at all! God is good!" I smiled.

"So, what are you doing? I have been saved for eight years and it has always been hard for me to find someone I could connect with, and I just really love your spirit," she said.

"Thanks girl, I was thinking the same thing about not having any saved women to hang out with. My best friend isn't saved and I'm hoping I can influence her by rubbing off on her. I'm not doing much of anything, just relaxing and trying to find a movie to watch. We're going to *The Wordz* tonight, you want to come?"

"Naw, I can't make it. I heard it was a nice restaurant with great poets. I don't like calling it a club though, it's nothing like one."

"Yeah, I love that spot, it's a place where I can just fade away from reality for a while, that and church, of course! Maybe you can go out there with us another night," I offered.

"Raven, is there something bothering you? I am not sure why I woke up today with you heavy on my mind." Kathy inquired.

My face changed suddenly. I didn't know whether I should tell her my marriage was ending or not. I've always been weary of telling too many people about what was going on in my love life because things may end up good again and they will always remember the bad. So I lied, Lord forgive me.

"Girl, things are going well. My husband and I were going to go out tonight but Shyla needed me so I told him we could go out another night. But we are good. Please just keep me in your prayers that things go even better than what they are going right now."

Kathy was quiet on the other end of the phone. She was the nursery worker at our church and her eyes lit up every time she looked at those young faces. She was a little bit older than I was, although I wasn't quite sure how old she was. She has never been married but when you question her about why she hadn't tied that knot yet, she'll quickly respond, "Girl, God ain't ready for me to get married yet. I'm still learning how to be a good wife. When I'm ready, He'll send me the one." Shyla had never met Kathy but I wanted her to. Kathy was a great influence on everyone around her and such an anointed sista. I've invited her to come along with me and Shyla to the poetry club quite often but each time Kathy refuses. I never understood why Shyla would get so angry when I would tell her I offered for Kathy to join us whenever we went out. I believed it was because Shyla knew she's full of the devil and didn't want to be around someone so anointed. I am hoping in time that I could get Shyla and Terrance to church so that they could know God the way I do.

"Hello, Kathy are you there?"

"Yes, I'm here. It's just that my spirit usually never lies. Well, nonetheless, let me pray for you and let you get back to your movie."

"Oh Kathy, that would be great!" I waited in anticipation.

"Father God, we come to you today to pray deliverance over your child, Lord. Raven is standing in the need of prayer, oh Lord. I pray strength, guidance and peace over her life, Lord. Free her mind, dear God. Bless her household and her husband. Allow her marriage to be stronger than ever, Lord. Open up Raven's eyes so that the things that should be revealed to her Lord, she can see. Remove any pain she may be feeling right now, and allow her to know that you are watching over her, Lord. Please forgive her sins, Lord, and come into her heart. Use me to be a light in her path, allow me to light any dark roads ahead, Lord. Bless our hearts, Father God. In Jesus' name we pray, Amen."

"Amen. Thank you so much Kathy. Thank you."

When I got off the phone with Kathy I stretched out across the couch and felt tears coming out of my eyes. I just lied to my friend about my marriage, but it was as if she could see right through me. I sat in deep thought. The nerve of Terrance to think that I would just accept his apology so easily! Like I would just see those stupid roses and forget that he hit me today, and forget that he had been treating me so cold. I didn't understand what I was doing wrong and why he just stopped loving me like he used to. Kathy prayed that God would reveal to me the things I needed to see, and I had been praying for the same thing. We've only been married a couple of years and I was hoping to be married for the rest of my life but at this rate, we'd be divorced before long. I knew God doesn't believe in divorce, but infidelity was definitely grounds for it. I always dreamed of having a husband, kids, and a big house with a pool and a dog. The only thing I had was a husband and not much of it. I brought up the subject of kids to him a year ago and Terrance practically laughed in my face. He said a baby would take away from his time at work and he felt like we just couldn't afford it right then. Terrance has his own studio on the west side of town and business is really starting to bloom. He felt a child would take his focus off of his business and force him to focus on home life instead.

I really wanted a baby! At least then I wouldn't be so lonely on nights when he had to stay late at the studio or when he went to his Music

Seminars out of town once every six months. I knew we made more than enough money but Terrance liked spending his money on new clothes, shoes and cologne. He had every bottle of cologne ever made and almost every pair of shoes created. Sometimes I think he's trying to keep up with Bill. Bill is a Talent Search Agent at Terrance's studio and is fine as all outdoors. He wears all name brand suits and is always sharp every time I saw him. Bill is married to a beautiful white woman and treats her like a queen. They've been married for over six years and I've never heard about any real problems they've had. When Terrance says he's with Donnie, I immediately doubt him. But whenever he says he's with Bill then I know for sure he's telling the truth because Bill is not the type to cover for Terrance. There were several times I overheard Bill pleading with Terrance that he shouldn't stay out so late and when he does, he needs to at least give me a courtesy call. Terrance usually just brushed off the comments and changed the subject.

When Terrance lied to me, most of the time I knew it was a lie but I just nodded my head and made a mental note. If I found out Terrance was cheating on me I would leave him with no problem but I just suspected it with no real proof. I didn't want to be the kind of woman to leave her man because she *thought* he's doing something. What if I'm wrong? What if he's just stressed out and needed time away from me? Yeah, well I knew deep in my heart that if that were the case then he wouldn't disrespect me like he does. I could try to make up every excuse in the book for him but it wouldn't change the facts. He takes my love and my kindness for granted.

I'd thought about making him wear a condom but didn't want him to say he'd stop having sex with me altogether. However, lately the sex with him hadn't even been as good as it used to be. It was almost like he didn't give a care in the world whether I was pleased or not, just as long as he got his. The only time the sex was any good was when he thought I was on the verge of leaving him, then he'd try to put his all into it to make me fall back in love with him. I'm not gonna lie, that junk worked but not anymore! We started only having sex once every two weeks and most of the time when that happened, it was because I initiated it. He doesn't even touch me and caress me anymore, and he even stopped kissing me while we're having sex. It was almost as if I were living with a stranger. I was tired of living my life for him! I needed to look internally to find out who Raven truly was. And I was determined to do just that!

I jumped up and decided that I'm going to go to *The Wordz* tonight looking the best I could. I wanted to turn heads and feel sexy again. Terrance never complimented me anymore but he usually just told me how hot he thinks other people looked. When I asked him how I looked then he'd always reply, "You look ok." I hated that! I put on a shower cap and jumped in the shower. I searched my closet frantically for the right outfit and I would let Shyla put my hair up in an up-do when she arrived. I was hoping that despite me feeling like crap on the inside, I would look like a million bucks on the outside. I hoped Terrance did come home early because I wouldn't be there. I'd be out having me a good time.

Chapter Seven

TONY: THE TOUR OF ORLANDO

Once I got home from work I laid down on my bed in exhaustion. I had a heck of a day! The weather had become very windy and stormy outside and it was at these times I wished someone was here by my side. The wind blowing outside made it sound like someone trying to break into my place, so I turned the TV on as a distraction. A karate movie was on and I have always loved karate.

'Ring!'

The phone rang five times before I managed to take my eyes off of the fight scene.

"Hello?"

"What's up my bro?" Ray was calling from Miami. Although it had only been a few days since I'd been up to Miami to see him, I missed him more than he realized. It was definitely time for a reunion of the Wilkerson brothers.

"What's up dawg? Let me tell you, the job I started is off the chain and it pays well. There's a fine honey here who wants to show me around this place but you know a brotha trying to show her around my pants." Ray couldn't help but laugh.

"You're a crazy man. I was calling to tell you that Shawna and I are getting married. I proposed just tonight and she said yes. Isn't that *great* bro?"

I couldn't believe what I was hearing. My brother was getting married. What on God's green earth would make a man want to do a thing like that? As many women as there were in the world, why choose to be with only one? I sat there on the phone in silence, totally speechless.

"Hello? Tony, are you there? Did you hear what I said? I'm getting married man and I want you to be my best man."

"Are you sure that's what you want to do, Rashawn? I mean, how long have you known this girl, two years? Can you really know a woman in two years of your life? I just don't want to see you ruin your life." He knew whenever I called him Rashawn instead of Ray, that it was a subject I was completely serious about.

Now there was silence at the other end. I suppose I should've been happy for him but I never understood the constitution of marriage. I just couldn't be happy for him, at least not at that moment. Ray had always had steady girlfriends and he always seemed to be the one getting hurt in the relationship. He was the type to fall in love extremely fast, and most of the women didn't feel the same way about him. The majority of his girlfriends ended up having a crush on me even though I was younger than Ray. Although I never messed with any of his girlfriends in the past, Shawna was different. Shawna was gorgeous and had these beautiful shoulder length dreads. The dreads were dyed light brown at the ends and gave her natural style a mysterious look.

Ray and Shawna had been dating for only two months when I first met her at a family gathering at Aunt Tina's house. I was looking better than ever and I felt her eyeing me the whole night. I didn't bring a date to the gathering because I knew that most of the single women would be checking me out. But that night, I was checking out Shawna. After a few hours of us staring each other down, I passed her a signal to meet me in the back room when the party had died down. I stood in the back room waiting for her to come back to talk to me.

"What are you doing back here? Are you waiting on me?" she grinned as she spoke.

I looked up at her beautiful brown eyes and whispered, "Yes, I wanted to know why you've been checking me out all night?"

Shawna looked a little nervous as she followed my eyes, trying to find out if I would scold her for flirting or embrace her.

"Well, I really wasn't checking you out but I think you were checking me out. I would like to know why, especially with you knowing that I came to this party with your brother."

Clever girl. I could tell she was trying to cover her tracks just in case I blasted her out.

"I like what I see and I would like to feel the things I don't see." I tried.

She hesitated for a second then cracked a smile as she looked around the room nervously. Ray had been drinking all night and was pretty smashed by the time the party had started. The house was quiet and the only noise you heard was the drip of water from the faucet in the kitchen. Aunt Tina had left and so had the last of the crowd. Ray was passed out across the floor in the living room so I ran to Ray's room looking for a condom. I hated those things, but I did not want to risk getting my brother's girlfriend pregnant. That would be the worst in my book.

"Well, is it safe?" she whispered anxiously.

"Yes, It is truly safe," showing her the condom I held in my hand.

She was wearing a shiny blue dress that came just above her knees with some shiny black high heels. I locked the bedroom door and threw her on the bed. My manhood was pounding so hard that I thought it would burst out of my pants. I was afraid we wouldn't have time to take all our clothes off so I just slid my hands up her dress and ripped off her panties. I could tell she wanted me bad because I could see a puddle of wetness on the sheet. As I went to put the condom on I stopped. *What the hell was I doing? This was my brother's girlfriend.* He told me the night before how he was starting to have feelings for this girl and here I was about to screw her brains out.

"What's wrong? Is someone coming?" She appeared to look confused and nervous all in one.

"I can't do this. You are definitely not the one for my brother."

She couldn't believe what she was hearing because she jumped up and pushed me off the bed. Tears fell from her eyes as she looked at me.

"I can't believe you did this to me, you set me up. Are you going to tell Ray?"

I knew I couldn't tell Ray because I was just as wrong as she was. I felt ashamed that I could even consider hurting my brother. I just stood up, pulled up my pants and shook my head as I walked out the room.

My thoughts were interrupted by Ray screaming into the phone, "Tony, Tony, Hello?!" I could hear Ray on the other end of the phone getting more and more pissed from my reaction so I took a deep breath and managed to tell him how happy I was for him. When we got off the phone, I turned the karate movie off and laid across my bed staring at the ceiling. Life had changed so drastically for me in the past year. Ray was settling down and it made me wonder if I'd ever feel that way about anyone. I'd met beautiful women in my past, some with degrees, some rich, some clever, and even some who were marriage material. I would never allow myself to open my heart up to them. Sometimes I wondered why I had this fear of commitment and why I was so afraid to love someone.

'Ring!' The phone was starting to get on my nerves.

"Hello?"

"Tony, Hi, this is Reigene. How are you?"

Ah, Reigene, what a wonderful voice she had.

"I'm fine and you?"

"I'm doing well. I hope I'm not disturbing you but I was wondering if you wanted to hook up this Saturday night to go sight-seeing?"

"I'd love to, wait hold on."

Someone was knocking at my door. When I opened the door I saw a chunky short black woman with old braids in her hair. She had on a long tee shirt and some baggy jeans with a blue choker necklace around her neck. She had a beautiful smile and beautiful dark brown eyes.

"Yes, may I help you ma'am?"

"Hello, my name is Monica. I'm your neighbor and I would like to welcome you to the apartments. If you need anything then I'm in apartment 319. What is your name?"

"Tony. Thank you for the offer. Actually, if you aren't doing anything Saturday then I would like to see Orlando a little more. Would you mind showing me around town?"

"Oh I would love to. I will tell my roommate I am taking you out and maybe she can come along, would you like to meet her?"

Uh, hopefully your roommate looked a lot better than you do, I thought. Maybe I could get a hook up.

"Sure! I'd love to meet her."

"We've been friends for about five years. She is very fun to hang out with but she has a man, so don't be trying to hit on her. This is not a hook-up session sir! This is simply neighbors showing another neighbor a night out on the town."

Well, at least I know that she must be a looker since she is warning me not to hit on her. I think Monica should be more worried about her roommate hitting on me.

"Of course not! That won't be a problem at all," I hoped.

"I will go get her and introduce the two of you and we will take you to see the town Saturday night."

As I closed the door I was relieved I could go sight-seeing with someone and not have to worry about whether or not I was going to score later. Besides, Reigene was an employee under my supervision and as tempting as it was, I didn't want to risk my job, well, at least not just yet. Just as I was getting me something to drink, I remembered Reigene was still on the phone.

"Hello, Reigene?"

There was silence on the phone. I suppose she hung up. As soon as I hung the phone up it rang.

"Hello, did you forget about me Tony?" she sounded irritated.

"Reigene, I'm so sorry. My neighbor came to introduce herself to me and I got distracted. She will be taking me out Saturday night to see the town. If you still want to take me out Friday night then I would love to make that happen."

"Oh, so you work fast. Ok, if I'm not going out with *my* neighbor Friday night then I will give you a call, see you at work tomorrow."

I sensed a bit of sarcasm and jealousy in her statement but I let it go. I was used to women getting jealous of other women I talked to or dated but I never paid it much attention because I told them all up front that I wasn't looking for a relationship. Nonetheless, when Friday came I told Reigene I just wanted to chill by myself and maybe we could reschedule. Saturday morning I went up the street to *Rainy's Gym* to join. When I walked in, I was impressed with how big the gym was. They offered light karate classes as well as weight lifting classes and I was anxious to start. I brought my workout clothes with me and started as soon as I signed the papers. I lifted weights and worked on my stomach for a while and headed back to the house. Later that night I threw on some jeans and a tight blue dress shirt to show off my muscles. I decided to wear my silver necklace and my favorite cologne "Joop for Men." I stared at myself in the mirror and thought *man I'm fine* and blew myself a kiss, which was right when someone knocked at the door. When I opened the door I saw this beautiful white woman with black curly hair and green eyes standing there. She had some straight pretty teeth and some big puffy lips and looked as if she could be Italian. Her shape was model-perfect and she was all dressed up wearing a blue silk blouse and a short jean skirt. I smiled as I thought *this must be my lucky night.*

"Hi, you must be Tony. I'm Sumner, Monica's roommate. I just wanted to see if you were ready and apparently you are."

Monica's roommate? She was gorgeous! I may need to slip her my number when Monica's not looking... naw, I'll be good!

"It's great to meet you. Monica seems like such a nice woman. I'm looking forward to going out tonight, where are we going?"

"Well, we were thinking about taking you to The Heights. It's an underground gathering spot where a lot of the clubs, restaurants and hang-out spots are located. You'll love it, I know."

Monica walked up as we were talking. She had her braids pinned up and they actually looked like something worth seeing. She had on a long brown dress with some brown heels and a brown and white choker. I looked at the two of them together and they looked like such an odd couple of friends.

"What's up Tony, you ready?"

"All ready! Let me grab my keys. Who's driving?"

"We will. This is your night." Monica stated.

They drove Sumner's black Ford Explorer with black leather seats inside. The radio was set on the reggae station and the windows were all tinted. I looked all around Orlando while we drove and it seemed no different than Miami.

"Are we going to Universal Studios as well?" I asked impatiently.

"Relax, we'll let you out the car soon enough. Any new resident of Orlando must see other things besides Disney and Universal Studios, and they should definitely see The Heights. We are going to The Heights, and then another night we'll go to the other hot spots; we can't see Orlando all in one night." Monica sounded more excited than I was to take me to the different spots located in The Heights a little outside of Orlando. There were about ten restaurants, clubs and live bands playing outside. It was all surrounded by water and I felt this calm feeling as if I never wanted to leave this spot. I could come down here each weekend and spend time in a different spot each time I came.

"I wish I had my camera. This is great! Ray would love this place."

"Who's Ray, your boyfriend?" Monica had this big smile on her face that showed all her teeth.

"Oh, you got jokes? I love women, don't get it twisted. Anyways, Rashawn is my brother and best friend. Maybe one day you will be able to meet him, I'm sure he'll be coming to visit me soon."

"I'm looking forward to it," stated Sumner.

We sat on the bench at the peak of The Heights by the water and got to know each other better. Monica seemed like the one I connected with the most and someone I could easily talk to. I told them all about my life of non-committed relationships and my only heartbreak. Monica seemed to be disgusted with my theory on "love them and leave them" but she just shook her head and said "men!" Monica explained that love should be cherished even when it's a hurtful thing. This led her to talk about the first time she realized she was in love. She was thirteen and her next-door neighbor came over quite often to hang out with her. His name was Jersey and the two of them were becoming best of friends. One night Jersey leaned in and kissed her and she pulled away. He was so embarrassed that he just kept apologizing and left. For about two weeks Monica avoided talking to him because she felt a tingle when she kissed him and it scared her. On that second week, she walked up on him kissing some cheerleader at their school. She felt herself get sick and extremely jealous. She felt betrayed, although she had pushed him away. She spent the rest of the month moping in her room after school, and not answering his calls. She realized then that she had fallen in love with him.

"Well, what ever happened with him and the cheerleader?" I inquired.

"He's married to her now! I'm still mad about that!" Monica laughed as she pouted.

Sumner jumped into the conversation occasionally and stated that love can be displayed in other ways other than in a romantic sense. She went on to talk about the love she had for her natural mother after she found out she was adopted. She finally located her real mother a couple years ago and was surprised that she was in a mental institution for having chronic schizophrenia. Sumner built a relationship with her mother as much as she could and often visited her but she also expressed a high concern about her mother's illness possibly being hereditary.

"Ok, enough serious talk, let's have some fun!" Sumner jumped up trying to hide the tears forming in her eyes.

"It's time for you to see the clubs!" she yelled.

There was a beautiful lake surrounded with boats that caught my eye as we walked away from the bench. I wish Miami had something like this; it would be amazing! Now if they had a poetry club here then I knew I would be in heaven. Lots of places have poetry clubs during the day or just on certain days but I inquired about it anyway.

"This is beautiful y'all! They wouldn't happen to have any poetry spots anywhere down here, would they?"

"They have everything down here, man. There's this place called *The Wordz* and I think they got something going on tonight. Do you do spoken word?" Sumner inquired.

"Yes, it is one of my greatest passions."

"Monica writes poetry as well, y'all should hit it off great." Sumner smiled at Monica as if she admired every piece of poetry she'd done. I could tell the two of them were very close friends, more like sisters, if anything else. It felt like I was with old friends as we headed over to the spoken word place. When we got to *The Wordz* I was very impressed with the size of the place. The *Lighthouse Club* in Miami wasn't nearly as large as this place was. Apparently they had more than just poetry there because of the different posters hanging on the walls and the box office booth in the corner that seemed to be closed for the night. When we walked in, I noticed how packed the place was with all kinds of nationalities and I found myself excited. There were tables set up all over the place and waiters dressed in uniforms with letters all over it.

"They serve food here?" I asked overly excited.

"Yep, they sure do! This is the spot to be at on Thursdays and Saturdays. All the other nights they have special events and people usually rent the place out."

Sumner was always so informative. She seemed to know the scoop on everything going on. I did my normal routine - scanned the room looking for the woman I was going to take home and impress with my poetry and there she was. She was a very beautiful light brown woman. Her hair was pinned up off her neck and she had on this tight red dress with this beautiful silver necklace. She was sitting with another beautiful woman with long black hair and she looked like a model of some sort. Normally I would approach the model but it was just something about the other woman that made me want to take her right then and there. She had this radiant elegance about her that would make a man want to melt all over her.

"Ladies, I see some eye candy. I will be back with y'all in a second."

Monica and Sumner looked at me and shook their heads.

"I tell ya, you just won't ever stop chasing women will you? Where is this eye candy you see anyway?" Sumner looked all around.

I pointed slightly over toward the two women sitting on the side of the room. "Well, you do have great taste but which one will be your candy?" Sumner asked.

"The one in red. Isn't she lovely?"

"She's beautiful, not as beautiful as I am though! Fortunately for me, I'm taken." Sumner winked at me and gave me thumbs up.

Monica seemed a little bothered by the conversation Sumner and I were having so I decided to cut it short and head over to get a taste of my candy. The two women were laughing hysterically as I walked over to introduce myself.

"I have never quite seen someone as beautiful as you." I looked at the lady in red and she smiled so elegantly.

"Are you talking to me?" She looked at her friend in a shy way and then back at me.

There was something so remarkable about her that made me unable to take my eyes off of her. I got this feeling in my stomach the moment she looked up at me, and I had never felt that before.

"You are the one. I'm Tony Wilkerson and you are?" *Whoa wait a minute. I just told this girl my real name. What's up with that?*

"Uh, I'm Debra, Debra Williams."

Her friend gasped loudly after she said her name for some reason and then turned to me, looked me up and down and smiled as she spoke.

"Hello, I'm Shyla. Are you a poet?" she inquired.

"Yes, I am. And you?"

"No, not really but my friend Raaa…" then she cleared her throat and repeated her sentence.

"No, not really but my friend Debra is. Maybe she will read something for you tonight. She's single and looking for someone nice. Are you looking for a good time?"

I didn't know how to quite respond to that and didn't understand why the hell I was talking to Shyla and not to Debra so I looked at Debra when I answered.

"I am looking for a great time, how 'bout you?"

"Uh, I am looking for something but I just don't know what yet." Once again Shyla sighed and took over the conversation.

"Who are those two women you were sitting with?" Shyla asked aggressively. Normally I like aggressive women but not when I'm trying to holla at the other one.

"Relax, those are just my neighbors. They are best friends and one seems like a man-hater and the other one is taken. Besides, I want you, Debra." Debra put her head down and blushed like a little child.

"Well, why don't you read something for us? They are waiting for someone to go on next."

"I will read something just for Debra." I winked at Shyla and blew a kiss to Debra.

I walked away from them and looked over at Monica and Sumner. Sumner was grinning from ear to ear while Monica continued to shake her head. I walked up to the host and told him I planned on going next. The man reciting his poem at the podium seemed a little disturbed while he read about his feelings on racism. I sat there and listened without trying to get depressed and waited patiently for my turn. He received a standing ovation when he was done and then the host introduced me as "Tony, the one and only." *I liked it.* When I stood at the podium I felt a little butterfly in my stomach as I looked solely at Debra.

"This piece is for Debra, the most beautiful woman in the room. It's called "My Favorite Instrument." I cleared my voice, looked straight at her and began.

"After studying her head to toe,
Her body I stroked like an instrument.
The music we made was amazing as I displayed my mastery of her rudiments.
Long and short notes....
Fast and slow strokes provided for a groovy rhythmic piece.
I caressed her body,
Finessed her entirely...
Like my piano keys.
A love harmony of affection, intimacy and passion.... echoed
As if I was holding her in my arms on stage, eyes closed...
Just sax'n.....
With my lips gently pressed against the mouthpiece
I use only the tip of my tongue
To moisten the reed
The vibrations from that combination sparked a sound I couldn't believe.
In tune, with perfect pitch, this last note peaked ecstasy.
Long winded indeed, her horn screams as I play my heart out,
Until I can no longer proceed.
I let her breathe....
Deep breaths of satisfaction bring a calmness to our melody.
The beating of our hearts pound heavily...
We just made beautiful music.
Me, the composer.
And you, my favorite instrument."

All the women were on their feet screaming and cheering when I finished. Debra stayed in her seat with this girlish blush on her face but Shyla was one of the main ones screaming. I'm sure I could get any girl in there including Shyla if I wanted to but for some reason I was extremely attracted to Debra. I always thought it was more appealing if a woman wasn't throwing herself at me because it gave me something to work towards. I loved a challenge. Instead of walking over to Debra I walked back over to Monica and Sumner smiling.

"So, what do you think?" I asked.

"I think you made just about every woman in here fall in love with you. Nice job! What happened with ole girl?" Sumner glanced over at Debra while she talked.

"She seems a little shy which normally wouldn't bother me but her friend kept interfering with my game. I think I'm going to do something I've never done before."

"And what might that be Mr. Playboy?" Monica asked sarcastically.

"I'm going to give her my number. I'll see if she calls and when she does, I will screw her and get rid of her."

"You are such a pig, Tony." Monica seemed a little irritated by my comments but I could care less.

"Monica, relax girl. Tony is just being a man, luckily my man would never let such disgraceful words come out his mouth!" said Sumner.

"Goodness! Monica is a man-hater and you are over here worshipping your man. He is probably out with some chick right now!" I snarled at Sumner.

Monica had to laugh at that one and smacked her lips. Sumner, on the other hand, didn't find that comment funny at all and just rolled her eyes. I had finally bought a cell phone and was anxious to give it out. I grabbed a napkin and wrote down my number and signed it *Tony, the one and only.* When I got up to give the number to Debra, I noticed they were gone. I ran outside to the parking lot and saw her getting into her car.

"Debra. Debra," I yelled. *Why am I running after this woman?* I had no idea!

She looked back and saw me and dropped her keys. When she bent down to get them I took a look at her fine round bottom. *Whew, I've got to have it!*

"Hey baby, you leaving so soon?"

"Yeah, I've got to be heading home. I really enjoyed your poem." She said with a blush.

"I'm glad, it was just for you. You are so beautiful, has anyone ever told you that?"

"Not lately, but thank you. I really have to be going! It was nice meeting you Tony."

Whoa, she's not trying to get with me and I'm just not used to this kind of treatment. I looked at her finger, no ring. So what was the problem? *Maybe Shyla was her lover, seems like I'm running into a lot of those lately, but then again it seemed like Shyla was trying to set her up with me.* I was confused.

"Where's your friend?" I inquired.

"We rode in different cars and she went to another club. Are you interested in her?"

"Hell no! You are the one I want. Let me give you my cell and house number. Call me whenever you want and if the voicemail picks up then please leave me a message."

I gave her my numbers and she took them hesitantly.

"Tony, do you know Jesus?"

What? I was not expecting that question from her and I became speechless. I just stared at her for a moment.

"Excuse me?" I pretended not to have heard the question.

"Do you know Jesus?" she repeated.

"Well, I am aware of Him. I have a lot more to learn. Do you know Him?"

"Yes, I do. He is awesome! You should really get to know Him; He can change your life completely. It was nice meeting you, Tony."

Once again, I was speechless as I watched her get in her car and wave as she drove away. *What am I doing here in the middle of the parking lot waving goodbye to a beautiful woman? Why was I suddenly wishing that I knew Jesus?* Perhaps we could've talked a little longer had I did. There was just something about that Debra woman that made me want to know more.

Chapter Eight

RAVEN: THE NIGHT OUT

I must have changed my clothes a million times before I found the dress I wanted to wear. It was a tight fitting red dress that Terrance bought for me a couple of years ago and the one I originally laid out to wear in the beginning. *Perfect!* I put on my red heels and my silver necklace. Terrance hadn't called all day and I was glad. If he did come home earlier than he planned then I wouldn't be here. I stood in the mirror and stared at this stranger looking back at me. What happened to that woman who was full of life and so much stronger? The moment a man would do me wrong I would just walk away from him in a second. Why was it so hard for me to walk away from Terrance? Was it because of the vows we said to one another? No one had ever treated me so cold. Maybe I just didn't wait on God, maybe I rushed into marrying a man who just wasn't the one for me. Just as a tear was forming in my eye the doorbell rang.

"Hey girl, bout time you got here." I stated.

Shyla looked beautiful as ever with her long black hair. She was wearing her short black mini skirt and white blouse. She had some beautiful legs and I sometimes found myself envying her for having that *I don't care* attitude. I wished I had that attitude, especially now.

"Girl you look great! Maybe you'll find you a man that will do you right, instead of that loser Terrance."

I just looked at her and changed the subject. I was always good at changing the subject.

"Are you going to pin my hair up or what? I just want something simple, as long as it's off my neck."

While she was pinning my hair up she went on and on about how she was starting to get serious about Justin. She stated that she was actually thinking about marriage. I couldn't believe my ears. For the past six months she had been like a totally different person, always turning down all the fine guys trying to get with her and calling home every so often to check in with Justin. I really liked Justin and they were perfect for each other. I just hoped Shyla was really as serious about him as she claimed to be. I didn't want her to hurt that man.

"There, all finished. Now let's go. Are you going to read tonight?" She asked me that every time we went to *The Wordz*.

"No, I'm not in the mood to read, how 'bout you?" I knew Shyla had never read a poem or even written one before but things were changing so much that I just needed to ask.

"Oh, you got jokes? You know I don't do all that. I wish we would go to a booty-shaking club but you're too holy for that now! Man, I wanna dance. You sure you wanna go to *The Wordz*? We can go to *The Spot*, I heard it be jumping on Saturday nights."

"No, Shyla, you know that I don't do the club scene anymore! I need to talk and get my mind off things. I actually would love for you to go to my church with me in the morning."

"Ha! Yeah, maybe one day but tomorrow ain't the day! Let me put this brush back in your room."

"No, wait!" Shyla had already walked in my room before I could stop her. I didn't want her to see the roses Terrance sent me.

"What the hell is this? Oh no that fool didn't try to make up by sending you flowers. That's the oldest trick in the book and I know you're not falling for that bull, are you?"

"Of course I'm not Shyla, that's why I'm going out tonight. I won't be here when he gets home, so let's go."

Shyla took the roses and threw them in the trash.

"Now we can go!" she smirked.

We took separate cars because I always learned from my mistakes. One time Shyla and I went out to a club and she met some guy and spent the whole night talking to him. We were supposed to leave by midnight but it was going on 1:00 A.M. before she even checked back in with me. I would've just left but of course I rode with her. When I told her that she knew I needed to be home by midnight, she apologized and told me to take her car and she would find a way home. Usually when we planned on going to one spot, Shyla always wanted to go to another club afterwards. She had already talked about how she wanted to go dancing tonight, so I decided to drive my own car. We met up in the parking lot of *The Wordz* and stood outside talking for a second.

"Girl, I love you. I just wanted you to know that, Raven. You are such a good friend and I know that I'm always putting Terrance down but it's only because I want what's best for you," she put her arm around my shoulder.

"I know Shyla and I love you too. I am happy you are here!" I smiled.

When we walked in *The Wordz* it wasn't as crowded as it normally was but there was a good little crowd. We got a table over in the corner and ordered drinks. A couple of poets had gone up and recited their poetry while I told Shyla how hurt I was about my marriage.

"Shyla, I took my ring off when I got in the car. I just don't know if I can stay married to this man."

"And you shouldn't Raven. I mean, what does that man have on you? I want you to promise me that no matter what he does, you won't take that fool back."

"I can't promise you that Shyla. I love that fool. I want to do what God wants me to do. I have to seek Him in all that I do. Terrance is all I've known for the past three years and I just can't imagine my life without him. I just don't know what I have to do to make him love me like he used to. I tried suggesting counseling at my church, but he won't even go to church with me so I should've known he'd refuse the counseling. It's as if I'm the only one fighting to save this marriage. Oh wait! I wanna hear this chick's poem."

The lady at the podium was dressed in all white wearing something like a sheet of some sort and did a piece on taking back her sanity. It was very deep and when she finished, I felt as if she had just read my mind. I needed to take back my sanity but I just didn't know where to start. As soon as the woman finished her poem, Shyla continued our conversation without skipping a beat.

"Well, if you are going to stay with him then I think you should at least do to him what he is doing to you. Find you someone you can call up when Terrance wanna act up. Get you some sex from someone else and once that man do it to you the right way then you will forget all about Terrance and you won't have any problem leaving his butt when he stay out all night. Is Terrance that good in bed that you don't want anyone else?"

"Terrance used to be good in bed, but now it's just wham bam thank you ma'am and he turns over and go to sleep."

I was told to never discuss your sex life with your friends but I didn't see any harm in her questions. I noticed the disgust on her face as I continued.

"Nonetheless, Shyla, I am faithful. Do you know the meaning of that word?" Shyla ignored the question and scanned the club.

"Girl look, there's a fine brotha over at the far right table. Too bad he's with those chicks."

I looked over to where Shyla pointed. Whew! That man *was* fine. He was bald headed with a tight muscle shirt on and some dark blue jeans. He was standing up by the table where two women sat. One was a chunky black woman with braids and the other was a beautiful white woman who looked like an Italian model. As beautiful as she was I assumed that she was the lucky woman. As I was checking them out, I noticed him looking over at us and I froze up.

"Shyla, girl he's looking over here. Maybe he wants to holla at you."

"Holla at me? He might want to holla at you! You're looking good tonight girl. If I was a lesbian, I'd try to holla at you."

We burst out in laughter at that ridiculous remark Shyla made. When I looked up the guy was right there at our table. I felt butterflies all in my stomach. *Man, he was fine.* I just knew he wanted Shyla but to my surprise he introduced himself to me first.

"I'm Tony and you are?" he asked.

I couldn't think and before I knew it I was introducing myself as Debra. *Debra? Where in the world did that name come from?* Lord, I'm trying to live right and I'm sitting here lying! I just didn't want to give him any of my information. I was a married woman even though I didn't have my ring on. *Oh my goodness, that smile of his was just out of this world and those thick eyelashes, oh my!* He was brown skinned and his bald head was shining and glistering. He had these muscles to die for and the sexiest deep voice. *What did he see in me? Why was he talking to me and not Shyla? Was it pity?* Terrance told me that no one would want me after he's done

84

with me. Guys tried to talk to me all the time at work or when I was out and about but none who looked like him and enjoyed poetry like I did. I could barely speak and I supposed I didn't have the right answers Shyla wanted me to have because she continued to intervene and speak for me.

"Who are those two women you were sitting with?" Shyla asked in such a *tell me now* tone. Actually, I was glad she did the talking so I wouldn't look like such an idiot. A frog was in my throat and my stomach was filled with a million butterflies. I felt like I could go home with this guy and rock his world if he tried hard enough but I just couldn't cheat on my husband and I didn't want to backslide. I knew it was nothing but the devil, and I was battling with my flesh. Tony seemed to be overwhelmed by Shyla and every time he tried to talk to me, she'd answer. She almost slipped up and called me Raven at one point but luckily she caught herself. She managed to find out who the women with him were, and I was a little relieved to find out they were his just his neighbors. Once Tony expressed he was a poet, Shyla came right back at him.

"Well, why don't you read something for us? They are waiting for someone to go on next."

"I will read something for Debra."

When he walked away, Shyla and I grabbed each other's hands and screamed.

"Girl, that's the answer to your prayers. You better get on that or I will."

"What girl? What about Justin?"

"Girl, I'm just joking but you better jump on that." I hushed Shyla up as I listened to the last part of Johnny's poem about racism. Johnny was a regular there and he always moved me with all of his deep pieces. As soon as he was done, Shyla asked, "Do you even know where Terrance is now?"

"No, maybe he's home."

"If he was home then he would've realized you weren't home and tried to call you by now," she said making her point.

"Regardless, I can't and won't talk to Tony and you need…" just as I was about to finish my sentence I heard his voice on the microphone.

"This piece is for Debra." *Oh my God!* We sat listening intensely. The poem he read made me wish I was single again. He went on and on about his instrument of love. For a vast second I thought about what it would be like to have Tony on the side. After Terrance was done breaking my heart I didn't think I would have room for anyone else. But on the other hand, I didn't want to be someone's one night stand after I'd gone through such heartache with Terrance. I knew that God would never bless me if I did wrong in my marriage. However, I was still flattered by Tony's words and actions.

When he finished his poem, all the women stood on their feet, including Shyla and a couple gay men and they all whooped and hollered. I just sat there afraid of what he would say to me next but then the weirdest thing happened. He didn't come to our table. Instead he went back over to his neighbor's table. I definitely wasn't expecting that considering the fact that he blew me a kiss right before he recited his poem and the poem was dedicated to me.

"What is this crap?" Shyla apparently noticed it as well.

"I don't know. Maybe he was just playing around with me. Could've been that he saw a girl wallowing in self-pity and just wanted to make me feel better. Let's get out of here. I need to get ready for church in the morning anyway."

"Well, you know I'm going to *The Spot,* right? Maybe one Sunday I'll go to church with you, but I don't know when that will be. Let me ask you something. Would you have talked to him if he came back over here? Maybe he'll be back, let's stay."

"No, I wouldn't and I don't even want the temptation of talking to him. So let's get out of here. I'll meet you in the parking lot of *The Spot*."

We split up in the parking lot and when I spotted my car I grabbed my keys out of my purse. I couldn't believe how fine that guy was and that he chose me over Shyla. I must admit it made me feel good. Usually if there was only one guy and the two of us were together then Shyla would be the lucky one that night. I thought I was pretty but I just didn't think I was as stunning as Shyla nor did I have that confidence she carried. Just as I was getting closer to my car I heard a man yelling for some girl named Debra. He yelled "Debra" twice before I remembered that was my name for the night. When I turned around it was Tony and I got so nervous all of a sudden that I dropped my keys. When I picked them up I mumbled to myself *"what am I going to do?"*

"You're leaving so soon?" He had these light brown eyes that seemed to gleam as he spoke to me. I tried to hurry him off by telling him I was heading home and then he asked about Shyla. I wondered why. Maybe he was getting tired of me acting like I didn't have time for him and wanted to try his chances with her. I nervously put my keys in the door when he reached over to hand me his number. I started praying after I took the number and before I knew it I was asking the poor man if he knew Jesus! Of course that was important to me but I didn't want to come off as being holier-than-thou either. The words just flowed out of my mouth telling him how awesome my God was. My hands were shaking so bad when I waved goodbye to him. I drove off and headed to *The Spot* just to make sure Shyla got there safely. When I pulled up, she was standing outside talking to some dingy looking white guy.

"Where you been, girl? Dave here was telling me about a show he's promoting next weekend, a male revue. We have got to check it out girl."

"I have my own male to review. I'm about to go, I just wanted to come over here to give you a hug and to tell you what just happened." I grabbed her arm and pulled her away from Dave and over closer to my car.

"What just happened?" Shyla was always so impatient.

"Tony stopped me outside before I got in my car and gave me his number girl." I pulled out the napkin he wrote the numbers on. Shyla screamed.

"Girl, you better call that brotha tonight."

"I can't girl. I don't even want to keep it, what if Terrance finds it?"

"You better put that junk in your cell phone under the name of Tonya and shut up."

I laughed at the thought but it was a good idea. Maybe I would keep the number just in case.

"So, what did you say to him?" Shyla inquired.

"Girl, you know I was so nervous, I just started telling him how good Jesus was, all the while praying that I don't fall victim to my temptations."

"I know you're joking right? Tell me you're joking, Raven."

"No, Jesus is very good and Tony didn't know Him like he should. Maybe I had an effect on him. There should never be a time where I am ashamed to talk about Jesus. Besides, if I was to ever move on from Terrance I would want someone who loves God as much as I do."

"I am not even going to comment on that. You know how I feel when you start talking all religious. You used to be cool to hang out with but now I can't even go into the club with my girl because she's talking about going to church in the morning! What kind of mess is that? Let's go in and dance girl, please just this one time." Shyla had this desperate look on her face but I refused. Besides, Shyla knew all the new dance moves and she was always the better dancer out of the two of us. I really just enjoyed listening to the music and watching others dance more than actually going out on the dance floor, but this night was different. That type of music was no longer appealing to me and I had bigger fish to fry.

"Are you going home after you leave here?" I wanted to make sure Shyla didn't fall into more temptation and cheat on Justin.

"Girl, Justin has been calling me all night leaving me messages but I haven't returned them yet. I am going to his house after I leave here, I just don't want him to cut my fun time short. Are you going home or are you going to call Tony and give him some?"

"For the last time, Shyla, I'm going home to my husband and to get my clothes together for church."

As I got into my car and watched Shyla walk into the club, I checked my cell phone. Terrance hadn't even called and it was going on midnight. Oh well, this was a night where I wanted to just hear from God. I took the long scenic route home with the windows down and the gospel station playing softly.

I ended up stopping my car near a small lake and got out to clear my mind. I thought about everything I'd gone through in my marriage and even prior to. I had a long talk with God about the way I needed my life to be. I was a little disappointed that Terrance hadn't even called me all night, and another hour had just passed.

I had to admit that the thought of being with Tony just to take my mind off of my problems was a nice one but I realized that I was someone's wife. On my way home I stared at my cell phone and then at the napkin Tony wrote his number on and thought about calling him. *I can't do it.* When I pulled up in the driveway Terrance's car was not there. My plan to be gone when he got home didn't work because he hadn't even come home like he said he would, nor had he called. All of a sudden I felt a burst of anger overtake me and I ran in the house and yelled.

"You asshole! I hate you, Terrance, I hate you!" I didn't even curse so I knew that the anger I felt was that of no other kind I'd ever felt. I ran to our room and grabbed a suitcase. I snatched all of his clothes off of the floor and threw them in the suitcase. I was in a rage and I never felt like that before. How dare he hit me, send me flowers saying he was sorry and he'd be home early and then not come home at all? He didn't know I was gone so there was no excuse and if he did come home and found me gone he didn't even bother to call me to find out where I was. I ran to the kitchen to grab some garbage bags and ran back in the room to fill the bags with his shoes, ties, cologne and all his other junk. "I hate you Terrance! Aaaaaaaaaaaaahhh!" I yelled, tears streaming down my face. Ok, I was starting to lose it but no one would witness me losing it other than myself so I didn't care. I was so frustrated and hurt by this man I called my husband. Just when I was grabbing his toothbrush I heard the door open and close. I stood there quiet for a second and all of a sudden I got scared of what was to come.

"Raven, where are you?" I just sat down on the bathroom floor and cried, not a normal cry but one of those hysterical cries. When he walked into the bedroom he yelled again, "Raven, where the hell are you?" He cracked open the bathroom door in our room and looked surprised to see me sitting on the floor sobbing. For a second he appeared to be at a loss for words as I looked at him with hate in my eyes.

"You packed my stuff, huh?" I just put my head down and sobbed a little more. He kneeled down on his knees and continued to speak.

"Raven, where were you tonight? I came home and you weren't here. I tried to call you but your phone must not have had a signal because it kept ringing and going busy. I called Shyla and left four messages on her phone, didn't she tell you?"

I looked up at him when he said that. Shyla had been checking her messages all night and not once had she told me he called. I still didn't say anything; I was just too hurt from it all.

"Baby, I know I've been doing you wrong and I'm sorry. If you can't forgive and forget then I will leave. I will leave now if you want me to."

I was still speechless and just put my head down when he got up and grabbed one of the bags. Then suddenly I jumped up.

"Terrance, no! I don't want you to go. Terrance please don't leave me. Please."

I couldn't fight back the tears and he dropped the bag and kissed me passionately. After a few seconds I pushed back.

"Terrance, why have you been treating me this way? What is it that I'm doing wrong? Please tell me and I will change it. I don't want to live my life without you. Come clean right now baby, are you seeing someone else?"

Terrance sat down on the bed and put his head down. When I walked over to sit next to him he began to talk.

"Raven, I have been seeing someone else. I don't know why I started in the first place. We went out to dinner a couple of times when I had to stay late at the studio and one thing led to another. I didn't mean to hurt you."

I couldn't believe my ears. This man was confessing to me and my heart was breaking at the same time.

"Who is she?" my voice cracked.

"It doesn't matter, Raven. All that matters is I have been seeing her for the past 4 months and it's starting to get serious. Well, *she's* starting to get serious and I think there will be drama sooner or later. After I hit you I realized my marriage was falling apart unless I did something about it. So I told her I wanted it to end and she got very physical and threatened to tell you so I decided to tell you first. I'm not going to see her anymore, Raven. Please give me another chance."

I just sat there in disbelief. *How could he do this to me?*

"Terrance, who is she?"

My hands began to shake. *Was she someone I knew? Was she prettier than I was?* My heart raced and it felt like my breathing was getting shorter and shorter.

"It's Sherry, the temp at the studio. I was working late about four months ago and Sherry stayed to help me. She had been flirting with me since she started with little comments here and there but I paid it no mind. After a while she ended up going to lunch with me a few times. Other times, when her car was in the shop, I offered to pick her up for work and drop her off at home. She always made sexual remarks toward me but I knew I was a married man and I had to stay within my boundaries. During the times when I was angry with you she always made herself available for me to talk to. The night she stayed late with me at the studio, she walked in with her shirt open and her breasts hanging out. She came on strong and I just couldn't control my temptation. I've been seeing her ever since. However, when I hit you I realized things were just getting out of control. I never wanted to hurt you, Raven, never!"

He started crying. I couldn't tell if those were crocodile tears or real tears but I was just in shock. I said nothing. Not only did he cheat on me but he cheated on me with a young white woman that just started working at his job. I'd seen her a couple times when took him lunch and she was a very pretty white girl. I did notice that she dressed provocative, which I thought was inappropriate with her working around a bunch of guys. I mentioned that to Terrance a few times and he said he couldn't tell anyone what they could or couldn't wear because he didn't believe in dress codes. She was around twenty years old and had always been friendly to me when I came to the job. I just couldn't believe what I was hearing. I couldn't believe it! Whenever I mentioned how pretty she was to Terrance, just to see what his response would be, he'd say she was just plain looking to him and that he wasn't into white girls enough to notice. Our marriage had been a lie. I just sat there and stared at him as he went on.

"When I went to break it off with her, she got angry and threatened to tell you if I left her alone. I couldn't let you find out that way so I decided to tell you myself. Even if you put me out then I wouldn't get back with her. Raven, I was serious when I asked if we could renew our vows. What do you think about all of this? Say something baby, say something!"

What was I to say? He cheated on me with some whore for four months. All the times he said he was at his boy's house or at his uncle's house, he was with her. I felt like going to the studio and slapping all the hell up out of her. I wished she would've tried to call me and tell me some mess about her and my husband simply because he tried to cut it off with her. She would've seen a side of me that even I didn't know I had. I was beyond hurt and extremely pissed. *But wait, who was that black woman who stopped us in the restaurant? She was surely black, was she a friend of Sherry's?* My mind began to race.

"Terrance, who was the girl in the restaurant? And be honest with me."

He looked at me and then looked away. When he finally answered I thought I would jump up and slap him.

"She was someone I slept with," he mumbled.

"Excuse me, I didn't quite hear you."

"She was someone I slept with."

"Slept with when, Terrance?"

"Within the past month, Raven." He saw the look on my face and then began to plea.

"Baby, listen, I have made mistakes and I'm sorry. I am trying to be honest with you because I love you. I didn't have to tell you about this other woman. I think I have a sexual addiction. I want to stop, baby, please help me stop."

"You are such an asshole!" He looked very surprised to hear that language come out of my mouth as I jumped up and grabbed my purse and stormed out the house. When I got in my car I drove off so fast you would've thought I was being chased. I had no idea where I was going but I had to get out of there. My cell phone started ringing and I knew it was Terrance so I didn't answer. *Who could I call this late?* I needed to talk to someone but I just didn't know who since I knew Shyla was with Justin. *How could he do this to me?* I've been so faithful to him. He had no idea the many times I'd been approached by men that could care less whether or not I was married, but my love for him gave me the strength to say no and to stay faithful. I drove down to The Heights and stood by the bench near the calming and peaceful water. I dropped to my knees and cried so hard that I thought my eyes would fall out. "Father God, help me, Lord. Help me, Father God, why? Why, Lord, why?" After a couple minutes of getting all my anger out through my tears, I pulled out my little pad I carried with me and I sat on the bench and wrote.

"Ain't no sense in smiling
(I don't wanna smile no more)
Ain't no sense in crying
(my eyes are red and sore).

Ain't no sense in laughing
(I don't wanna laugh no more)
Ain't no sense in hurting
(Gonna throw that pain out the door)

Ain't no sense in living
(I don't wanna live no more)
But ain't no sense in dying
(Can't find nothing to die for)

Ain't no sense in trying
(I've given it all I could give)
Ain't no sense in nothing
(But that's the way I have to live….)

Help me Jesus!"

I turned the page. For months Terrance had been sleeping with someone else and then coming home sleeping with me. I felt another tear come to my eye as I wrote one more poem.

"She was touched by the same hands that wiped my tears when I cried,
Held by the same arms that embraced my soul when it died.
She was kissed by the same lips that kissed my fears away,
Greeted by the same smile that got me through each day.
She was moved by the same words in which I stand-
The problem was – she was loved by the same heart that belonged to MY MAN!"

I felt a little refreshed after I wrote my feelings down and then I looked at the time. 2:34 A.M. *Who could I call this late?* I strolled through my cell phone book of numbers and ran across the name Tonya. That was the name I saved Tony's number under. Maybe he's still awake or maybe he's still out. He gave me his cell phone and his home number and I sat there for a second and thought *why not?*

Chapter Nine

TONY: BREAKING THE NEWS

Monica and I sat at the table at *The Wordz* while Sumner went to the restroom.

"So, did you get the girl's number?" she inquired.

"Naw, I gave her mine. She acted as if she's a suspect on *America's Most Wanted*. I don't know, Monica, but it's just something about her that I like."

"She *is* beautiful. Guys usually love beautiful girls." Monica looked around for Sumner and then continued.

"I don't really like when Sumner drinks and start flirting like she was trying to do with you on the sly. I promised Chris I would look out for him."

"I kinda felt that vibe from you when she was talking to me, but I didn't think she was flirting with me. Has she ever cheated on him before?"

"*Has* she? Plenty of times. She's come home sometimes with hickies all over her neck and smelling like straight liquor. We'd fuss about it and she'll either lie about it or just outright tell me the truth, as if she could care less. Chris is a minister at his church and he is so in love with her. I think she knows how much he loves her so she thinks she can just walk all over him. I'm just as good of a friend to Chris as I am to her so it's hard for me. For the past few months she told me that she's been trying to focus on being faithful to him and do the right thing by him. He is planning on proposing to her but it just doesn't sit right in my spirit knowing all the things she's done to him."

"Man, that's messed up if dude is thinking about proposing, that's why I stay away from things like that. She does appear to be a little flirtatious, like she was with the bouncer, but I thought that was just her personality."

"So, are you going to read another poem?" I wondered why Monica all of a sudden changed the subject when I looked up and saw Sumner walking toward us.

"Monica, why don't you read something?" Sumner asked.

"Sumner, I really don't feel like reading anything. Have you talked to Chris?"

"He called, but I let it go to voicemail," she answered.

"Sumner, you've been eyeing that guy over there all night, I told you that I don't get down like that. Chris is a good man and if you don't want him then you need to let him know."

This was about to go to a place I didn't want to be. Sumner just looked at Monica and laughed.

"You sure are a hater! I tell ya something, I don't give a damn how you feel about Chris! Maybe *you* should date him. You know what? I think that's what it is. I think *you* want him. You can't find a man of your own so you want mine. Ok, you go to wherever Chris is and if that man I've been *eyeing* all night wants to take me home then I'll go with him," she took another sip of her drink and got up and started walking over to the man sitting in the corner.

Monica put her drink down, stood up and grabbed her arm.

"Sumner, go to hell. I'll tell you one thing, if you go home with that man then I'm calling Chris first thing in the morning and telling him everything! Tony, let's go," she yelled over at me. Sumner, obviously intoxicated, headed straight over to the guy, sat on his lap and started laughing. I jumped up, looked at Sumner and shrugged my shoulders, and followed Monica out. By the time we got in the truck Monica was in tears. I had just met these chicks and had no idea what to say, besides, Sumner was acting the same way I would act. Monica was way too sweet and innocent and she expected everyone to be the same way.

"Are you going to be okay, honey?" I asked.

"Yeah, I'll be fine. I've been thinking about putting her out the apartment for the past few months now, but she promised me that she would change her behavior. I try not to get involved in her business but she involves me because she lives with me. I've threatened to tell Chris plenty of times but never have, so she probably thinks I'm bluffing. This time I promise you I'm not bluffing. Chris is a good Christian man and he deserves much better. Sumner and I live totally different lifestyles and I'm sick of this, Tony."

"Well, I understand how you must feel. Do you think it's a good idea to leave her here, though? How will she get home? That man may try to hurt her."

"Trust me, Sumner always finds a way home! The club closes at 2:00 A.M. so they are about to shut it down now anyway and she'll be able to find her a way home. She may call Chris to get her or she may go home with that man. Even if I insisted that she come home with us she wouldn't. Her lifestyle is dangerous! I don't like it and I can't put up with it. I'm putting her out and she will have to find another place to stay. Let's head out, do you want to go get something to eat?"

"I do but I just feel so tired. I don't know why because I took a nap earlier but my body feels drained. I think I'll just go back to the house."

On our drive back Monica went on and on about how she was going to pack all of Sumner's belongings and place it outside the apartment door. The apartment was in Monica's name so she had every right to do so. Monica seemed to be more upset about the way Sumner called her a hater and accused her of wanting Chris. Those words really bothered her and she made sure I knew that. When I got back to my place I hugged her, thanked her for a great night, and told her to take it easy. Once I got inside my place I couldn't believe how tired I felt. It was only 2:30 A.M. and usually when I went out I could hang until at least four or five in the morning. I laid on my bed and stared at the ceiling. Within minutes I was fast asleep.

'Ring. Ring'

I jumped up and looked around in a panic. The phone had startled me and I felt a little out of it when I answered my home phone.

"Hello?"

'Ring. Ring'

What the hell? It was my cell phone ringing. *Who was calling my cell phone at almost 3:00 A.M.?*

"Hello?"

There was silence on the phone until I said hello again.

"Tony?"

"Yes"

"Tony, it's me Debra. How are you? You sound like you were sleep. I thought for sure you'd still be out and about. I'm sorry if I woke you."

"No baby, don't be sorry. I didn't think you would call. I just got in not too long ago and dozed off. I'm awake now. So, tell me something good."

"What do you want me to tell you?"

"Well, you can start by telling me why I spent most of the night talking to your friend and not to you, what are you hiding?" I joked.

"I'm not hiding anything. I just got out of a relationship and I guess I'm not used to talking to other guys."

"You are so beautiful, girl. I normally don't give women my number but it's just something about your eyes that just makes a man melt."

There was silence on the phone again. When she responded I could hear the smile in her voice.

"You are too kind. Are you involved with someone?"

"No, I'm free. Would you like to stop by? We could talk more."

Yeah right talk more.

"No, I couldn't. It's pretty late and I gotta go to church in a few hours but you can take me out to dinner one night if you want to talk more."

Dinner? That would be almost like a date. I couldn't remember the last time I went out on a real date. I guess if I had to wine and dine her to get what I wanted, then I would.

"Dinner sounds great. Do you go to church every Sunday?" I inquired.

"Yes, I try to. I am so tired right now though, it's already 3 in the morning and I can't sleep. I may not be able to make it, but Lord knows I am going to try."

"I'm impressed. I haven't met too many beautiful women so dedicated to God. I would love to hear more about you and your journey with that. How about tomorrow night over dinner, say around 8:00 P.M.?"

She hesitated for a moment before she answered.

"Let's do it Tuesday night instead."

"Ok. Where should I go to pick you up?"

"Well, I will have to just meet you at the place you choose. I don't like anyone knowing where I stay right away, at least not until I get to know them better."

"I can understand that. So how will I get in touch with you to let you know where I made reservations? Can a brotha get your number?"

"No, I will call you around 7:00 P.M. Monday night to confirm."

"You will call *me*? Fine, call me at 7:00 P.M. Monday."

When we got off the phone I could barely keep my eyes open. I was hungry as hell and went in the kitchen to make me a sandwich. I had gotten excited just from hearing Debra's voice. She had this very sensuous voice, squeaky but sensuous. Just when I was about to make my sandwich, my hands began to shake and my eyes started to close so I just threw the bread on the counter and laid on the couch and fell straight to sleep. When I woke up the next morning I was lying in a puddle of sweat. The couch was soaked and so were my clothes. Other than feeling a little weak, I felt fine so I couldn't understand why I woke up in such a heavy sweat. I thought maybe I left the heat on but the air was on full blast. When I looked in the mirror there appeared to be small bags under my eyes. I felt a little scared at first but I just brushed it off as maybe I drank too much the night before. Although, there were times I'd been pissy drunk and never once had I awakened in such a sweat.

I was so hungry it felt like my stomach was touching my back. I didn't feel like cooking so I decided to go out somewhere for breakfast. I jumped in the shower and threw on a tee shirt, jeans and some tennis shoes. When I opened the door I looked down the hall and noticed Sumner's clothes were still sitting in front of the door so I assumed she never came home. *Maybe I'll wake Monica up so she can join me.* I knocked about five times before she opened the door. Her eyes looked worse than mine but I could tell it was because she had been crying.

"Baby, you ok?" I asked.

"Sumner didn't come home last night. She hasn't even called. Chris called me this morning worried about her because she has not returned his calls. I told him everything. We both cried on the phone. I felt very sorry for him. I know it wasn't my place but right is right and wrong is wrong."

"Well, I see you packed her bags. Does she have a place to stay now that you've outed her?"

"I don't know. Chris wants to talk to her but she may go stay with one of her other friends. I can't deal with it anymore, Tony."

"I hear ya. Hey, I'm starving! Why don't you go out to breakfast with me and we can talk about it." She agreed to breakfast and then I asked if she was just going to leave that girl's stuff out here in the hall.

"You darn right! She called me a hater when all I was trying to do was look out for her. Let me throw on something, come in."

When I walked in her place I was impressed with the décor. It was decked out with all African designs, pictures and statues. Over the entertainment center was a big picture of Monica and an older man with white hair. Monica had her braids out and what looked like a relaxer in her hair; she actually looked pretty. She had on a boyish red collar shirt with a big silver rope chain on her neck and no makeup on.

"Who's the guy in the picture?"

"Oh, that's my father," she said with a smile.

"Oh yeah, I can see the resemblance," I noticed their noses were the same.

"Man, you look like I feel. What's up with those bags under your eyes?" Monica stared at me as if she'd seen a ghost.

"Me? What's up with those red eyes of *yours*?" I responded back.

"You know I just didn't get any sleep but I know you did because you were so quick to go inside so you could crash or was that just a ploy just to get rid of me?"

"Naw, I don't know why I have these bags under my eyes. This morning I woke up in a puddle of sweat. Maybe I'm coming down with something."

"Well, don't give it to me. You ready?"

Monica took me to *Tom Wilsons* restaurant where they served breakfast all day and night. When we sat down Monica let out a sigh.

"Tony, what am I going to do? I'm not the most attractive woman in the world and if I had a man that was even half as good as Chris then I would cherish him. He has such a great personality and he is so fine! I love Sumner so much but I just can't continue to put up with this crap from her. I know she doesn't think it's my responsibility to say anything to her or to Chris, but I just can't help myself when I know that a good man is hard to find. How am I supposed to handle this, Tony?" Tears rushed down her cheeks as she let out another sigh and continued.

"I don't think I can take much more of this. I am about to lose my best friend."

Monica looked pitiful when the waitress walked over to take our order.

"Have I seen you before?" The waitress asked looking at Monica. Monica glared up at the waitress with red watery eyes.

"No, I don't think so." Monica immediately went back into staring in her menu and uttered, "I would like to order the bacon and eggs along with three buttermilk pancakes."

Something was going on here, and it was clear Monica tried to change the subject by ordering but the waitress continued on with Monica.

"Ok, I got your order. But I know I know you, isn't your name Monica?"

"No, that is not my name. Can you please take my man's order so we can eat?"

Her man? The waitress looked confused as she looked over at me.

"I'm sorry sir, may I take your order?" I must've had the same look of confusion on my face as she did because Monica kicked me under the table. After I ordered, the waitress walked away in a rushed manner. I looked at Monica and just when I was about to ask her what the hell that was all about, she burst out into tears, again.

"What's wrong? Why are you crying *now*? What is going on with all this *"no, I'm not Monica"* talk?"

"I'm sorry I'm so darn emotional. One night about four years ago I went to this club with Sumner. We had a blast and we danced all night and she got extremely drunk. I had to go to the restroom and when I came back out, Sumner was all over this white guy. I walked away from her and the guy's friend followed me. He was a very dorky looking black guy with thick glasses and a goofy laugh. He introduced himself as Burl and gave me a big smile. I was drinking a lot that night and all I could remember was telling him my name and kissing him. Before I knew it, I heard a woman's voice screaming, "Burl, how dare you do this to me?!" I looked the lady in the face and saw it was a girl from my high school, our waitress. She was shocked and hurt when she saw me and I just apologized and ran away. I was so embarrassed because I had never carried on that way, Tony. I felt so ashamed!"

Everything was making sense now, well sort of.

"Ok, are you sure you want to eat your food from her?" I laughed. Monica forced a laugh through her tears as she quickly wiped her face.

The waitress was sort of homely looking. She had a beautiful plain face with big round eyes. Her hair was cut really short but it wasn't curled and it was slicked down with gel or maybe hair lotion. She was really skinny and I noticed her flat iron board butt when she walked away. She barely had any breast, just a pair of knobs sticking out of her shirt. And the gap between her teeth didn't seem to take away from her warm smile. I really didn't understand what the attraction was that Burl had for her but she wasn't an ugly woman.

"I just want to apologize to her," Monica proclaimed.

The waitress brought over the food, not looking at Monica at all. She seemed as if she wished she could be anywhere else at that moment except there.

"Sir, is it too hot in here?" She asked me.

"Excuse me?"

"You are sweating a lot. If it's too hot in here then I could ask them to turn up the air conditioner for you."

I hadn't even noticed the sweat running down my forehead until she said something.

"Please don't turn up the air conditioner, I am cold already. I'm just making my man hot, he'll be ok." Monica winked at me after she spoke. The waitress didn't look at Monica at all and she just turned around to walk away.

"Kimberly, wait!" Monica yelled.

"Yes?"

"Remember that night some years back when you saw me kissing your boyfriend Burl? I am so sorry! I have been feeling guilty about that for so long. I didn't know he was your man and I was drinking a lot that night and feeling vulnerable. Please forgive me."

"It's ok, Monica, Burl explained the whole thing to me. He told me how he grabbed you and forced himself on you and you pushed him away. I do not hold grudges, girl and I got rid of that loser a long time ago. I figured it was you that night but I wasn't quite sure. It's been a long time since I've seen you prior to that night, you looked different."

"Yeah, I've changed a lot. How have you been doing?" Monica inquired.

I saw it was going to be a long girl conversation so I excused myself and walked into the bathroom. The bathroom was covered with toilet paper and paper towels thrown everywhere. I'd heard that the women's public bathrooms were always filthier than men's and by looking at how awful this one looked- I cringed at the thought of the women's bathroom across from this one. The smell of urine mixed with a touch of mildew was in the air as I made my way to the mirror. The back of my shirt was soaked with sweat. *What in the world is going on? Why am I perspiring the way that I am?* I took a paper towel and ran cold water on it and wiped my face. I was getting a little worried, this just wasn't normal. I made my way back to my seat where Monica was half way done with her meal. I was only gone for about five minutes.

"Gees, you must've been hungry with your greedy self."

"Yes, I was. You have a problem with that? You need to sit down and eat so you can catch up. Don't play with me when it comes to food. Are you ok?" she asked.

Monica finally had a smile on her face. Since we'd been here she hadn't managed to accomplish such a task.

"Yeah, I'm fine." I lied. I wasn't fine. I didn't know what was wrong but I knew something was. I had plans to make an appointment with a doctor as soon as I got a chance.

"I got a date Tuesday night with that girl I met at the club last night."

"Get out of here! I thought she wasn't interested, so she actually called, huh?"

"She called about an hour after we got home last night. She seems a little mysterious, but I like that. I will be tapping it after dinner though."

"Tapping it? Listen to your sick butt, you are so damn shallow. How come you can't take the lady out, have a great time and kiss her goodnight?"

"I *will* kiss her goodnight, right as I am turning over to go to sleep and I will kiss her good morning as well."

I took a big swallow of my soda and just blurted out what had been on my mind all night,

"So, how long have you had a crush on Chris?"

Monica nearly choked on her tea. Her eyes looked at me with a shocking, yet busted, expression.

"What are you talking about?"

"You know what I'm talking about, Monica. You have a crush on Sumner's man, admit it!"

She put her head down.

"Tony, I think that I am in love with him. I just don't know why or how it happened. Nothing has ever happened between us, but he's just the perfect man for me, not for her."

Monica and I sat at the table for about an hour after we finished our breakfast and talked. We talked about everything from work to Sumner to our plans for the next five years. I felt a strong connection with Monica because she was very easy to talk to and I could see us becoming the best of friends. She also seemed to be feeling a little better about the Sumner situation. I finally convinced her to just sit down with Sumner when she does come home and talk to her. On our way out of the restaurant Monica left a twenty dollar bill on the table with a note that read *please forgive me – Monica.*

When I got back to my place I jumped in my bed with all my clothes and shoes on and got under the covers. My body felt drained as I felt my eyes closing.

'Ring'

'Ring'

I heard the phone ringing but my body wouldn't allow me to get up and answer the phone. I heard the machine pick up.

"Hey man, this is your brother. I want to come see you next weekend so we can hang out like old times. Hit me up and let me know if that's cool with you. Peace."

I forced out a smirk as my eyes remained shut. Ray was finally coming to see me. Hopefully I would be feeling much better by then. I figured I'd sleep for a while and then get up to search for a nice restaurant to make reservations for. I must've fell into a deep sleep because when I woke up hours had passed. I spent the entire day in bed, watching television, writing and sleeping. When I finally got out of bed Monday morning for work, I heard my cell phone beeping in the living room to let me know I had messages so I jumped up and grabbed it. Reigene called saying she wouldn't be in for work, but no message from Debra. I was starting to wonder if she would stand me up for our date. I hoped not.

I spent the entire day at work in meetings getting a chance to meet all the big wigs. They all seemed pretty impressed with me so I was confident that I'd be moving up the corporate ladder quickly. As soon as I got home from work I got a call from Debra. I told her I planned on taking her to The Shimmer Bay Grill. I heard it was a beautiful and expensive restaurant. She seemed very excited about it but rushed me off the phone. It really didn't bother me much that she rushed me off the phone because I went straight to bed and passed out. I didn't know why I was sleeping so much. My appetite had diminished a little so I didn't eat dinner that night. I slept throughout the night and woke up Tuesday morning in a puddle of sweat. When I got out of my first meeting at work, I had a few messages on my phone. Two were hang ups and then the message I'd been waiting for, Debra.

"Tony, I really don't want to go out anywhere for dinner tonight." There was a pause, "maybe we can order in and eat at your place. How does that sound? I will call you back tonight around 7:00 P.M. to see if you are cool with that idea and what I can bring."

Her voice seemed fragile and rushed. *This was going to be easier than I thought.* I thought of the perfect setting: candle lights, champagne and soft music. After work I stopped at the grocery store because I wanted to cook for Debra. I felt energized suddenly and thanked God that I was feeling better. On the way out to my car I noticed that the bag of clothes sitting in front of Monica's place were finally gone. I contemplated knocking but decided otherwise because I didn't want to waste too much time and I knew how long-winded Monica could be. I decided I would talk to her once I got dressed and got the food started.

I got back to my place and rushed to prepare the perfect meal. Time seemed to be going faster than normal and I was starting to feel like a school boy on his first date. I felt excited and nervous all at the same time. This feeling was an unusual one that I hadn't felt in a long time but I must admit I liked it. As soon as I got out the shower I heard a knock at the door. When I opened the door, this tall dark skinned man with crooked glasses was standing there with an envelope in his hand.

"Yes, may I help you sir?"

The man cleared his throat before speaking.

"Mr. Anthony Wilkerson?"

"Yes, may I help you?"

"I live down the hall. This envelope was in my mailbox by accident. I wanted to make sure you received it."

As he handed me the envelope, I looked at the return address and it had Earlene Thomas-Brown's name on it with no address under it. I closed the door and ripped open the envelope and started reading the enclosed letter. It was a very short letter apologizing again for hurting me way back when and then it stated: 'I just wanted you to know that you have a child. He is ten years old and his name is Charles. I am not asking for child support, I only want to give you an opportunity to get to know your child if you want to. I will be in touch.'

What? I didn't know what to think or what to feel. After all that time how could she just spring this on me? I told her I would take care of my child if, in fact, it was my child, so why didn't she let me know way back then? I'd missed out on my son's childhood and now she wanted to tell me after ten years! I wondered if Charles looked like me. What the hell would I do with a ten year old son? I didn't know the first thing about being a father. Thoughts flooded my mind so I took in a deep breath and tried to get them out of my head.

At 7:00 P.M. I spoke to Debra, gave her directions and then headed down to Monica's apartment. I really needed someone to talk to about this child situation. It seemed like my world was slowly crumbling before my eyes. Right as I was about to knock on the door, it opened. Sumner was standing there with bags in her hand.

"Hi, Tony. I was just about to leave, Monica is inside."

"Sumner, what's going on? Y'all need to work this out. Are you leaving for good?"

"Yeah, our friendship is over. I went to Chris' house Monday and we had a big blowout. Our relationship is over and it's all because Monica doesn't know how to mind her own damn business. I came back here this evening to get my stuff and she had the nerve to have my stuff sitting out in the hall. The neighbor said it's been out there since Saturday night. Tony, I almost jumped on her."

"Monica is a sweet woman who happens to love you. She is just concerned about you and your safety. True enough, she probably shouldn't have told Chris anything about you, but she considers Chris a friend also. Imagine yourself in her position."

Sumner looked pissed as she dropped her bags.

"Tony, didn't we just meet you Saturday? You are really acting like you know a lot about me and Monica. You have no idea the stunts she's pulled to try to break me and Chris up. She's not that sweet young woman you think she is. Maybe you can take my place as a friend because I don't need friends like that!"

Monica must've heard us talking and ran to the door.

"What's going on?" she asked.

"Your friend Tony seems to be taking up for you. You got him fooled just like everybody else," Sumner yelled.

"Sumner, get the hell out of my house! I don't ever want to see you again. Now go!" Monica yelled.

"This shit ain't over! No one breaks up my relationship and get away with it!" She grabbed her bags and stormed out. Monica looked at me and shook her head.

"Tony, why did you even try to reason with that girl? We were arguing all evening; there's no reasoning with her. She had the nerve to blame me for breaking her and Chris up. This is all her doing! She spent the entire weekend with that guy from the club and Chris didn't hear from her until Monday."

"Wow! Are you going to be ok?"

"Yeah, I will be fine. I just have to get used to not having her here with me. But enough about her, you look much better than you did this weekend. You look nice, man! Where are y'all going for your date?"

"Well, I decided to cook. I made my famous homemade lasagna and I have some candles and champagne too. I was all excited about this date until I got slapped with this." I handed Monica the envelope. She read the letter with her eyes wide and mouth open.

"You have a child! Why is she just springing this on you now? What are you going to do?"

"I don't know! That's the girl I told you broke my heart when I was eighteen. She cheated on me with her ex-boyfriend and wasn't sure if the baby was mine or his. We had a big falling out and I never heard from her again. I heard shortly before the baby was born that she moved to North

Carolina to live with her uncle. I assumed the ex-boyfriend went with her. I don't even know how she got my address. I don't know what I am going to do but there's no return address so I guess I have to just wait 'til she gets back in touch with me. This is messed up though, Monica! What am I gonna do with a ten year old son?"

"Man, you are right! That *is* messed up, Tony, but you will be a good dad."

"I'm not so sure about that! But I will talk to you more about it later, I want to get back over there to my apartment and get things situated."

"Ok, keep your head up, my friend. And bring me some of that lasagna."

Chapter Ten

RAVEN: EMOTIONS

"Is that man finally gone, girl?" Shyla sat in my kitchen Tuesday morning as I told her about the confession Terrance gave me. I refused her calls this weekend and called out of work Monday and Tuesday. I just needed time alone to think.

"He's gone for now, Shyla. I slept in my car and stayed out 'til 8 in the morning Sunday. When I got home all his clothes were gone. My cell phone rang all night Sunday and Monday, girl, but I didn't answer it. After the twentieth time calling, he finally left a message last night talking about he's sorry he hurt me, and that he loved me. He said he wanted to give me time away from him so I could miss him. He said he's staying in a hotel alone. I didn't call him back and I won't be thinking about him tonight when I see Tony. He is taking me to a nice restaurant for dinner. I am so nervous."

"What are you wearing? You have to be a knockout tonight. You know I can't stand that Terrance, I'm so glad you got rid of him." Shyla smiled as she jumped up to fix some coffee. It was darn near 10:00 A.M. and she acted like I woke her up too early.

"Shyla, I haven't gotten rid of him. I love him, I am hurt, yes, but I am not ready to just give my marriage up. Anyway, I don't know what I'm wearing tonight, you have to help me pick out something. He's taking me to the *Shimmer Bay Grill*, it's so expensive and beautiful in there."

"*The Shimmer Bay Grill?* Isn't that the place Terrance's cousin goes to all the time?" I looked up at Shyla in horror, she was right. How could I take another man to a place where I might run into Terrance's side of the family?

"Oh my God, girl, I forgot all about that. What am I going to do? I can't let anyone see me with another man, especially not this soon."

"Raven, I wouldn't give a damn if Terrance saw you himself. After all the things he's done to you, why do you care? What we need to do is go to his studio and beat that hoe ass, let him see that."

"You are so crazy! I might end up killing someone so I will steer clear from her for a while until I cool down. And I do care if he sees me because regardless he is still my husband. Maybe I should just tell Tony I can't make it." Shyla gave me this *'I can't believe you just said that'* look.

"Look, Raven, go out with Tony. He is just what you need, even if nothing happens then he will at least help you get your mind off of Terrance for a while. I tell you what, if you are worried about someone seeing you then call him and tell him you want to order in, he does have his own place right?" She winked at me as she searched through my refrigerator for some yogurt. I guess she was right, ordering in would make me feel a little more comfortable but I didn't want him to think I was easy or trying to get close to him, what if he tried something with me? Maybe I should just let him know up front that this was just a date and nothing more. I picked up the phone while I paced back and forth wondering if I was doing the right thing but I said *what the hell* and called his cell. Just as I was about to leave a message, I got nervous and hung up. I tried once again but hung up again. *This is just crazy!* Terrance had been sleeping with at least two women and I acted as though I couldn't eat in at a man's house.

I called a third time and finally left a message letting him know I wanted to cancel the restaurant plans and just order in. I also let him know I would be calling him back later to get directions. When I hung up the phone I held the phone to my chest and prayed out loud, "Dear God, forgive me." Shyla just shook her head and started in talking about Justin.

"Justin wants me to move in with him, Raven. He just came out the blue and said it, I don't know if I'm ready for that."

"Well, you are always there with him, anyway! It's almost as if you live there already. What would be so different?"

Shyla turned her head to look out the window. I could tell she was worried because it was written all over her face. She shrugged her shoulders and kept silent. I couldn't believe she wasn't jumping all over that offer since she was always talking about how much she loved Justin. I sat down at the table and grabbed her hand.

"Shyla, what's wrong?" I waited impatiently for the answer. She looked at me with tears in her eyes.

"Raven, what if I can't do it? What if I fail at making him love me? What if we end up like you and Terrance?" I gave her a sour look.

"Gee, thanks, Shyla."

"No, you know what I mean. I don't know if it's him or me that I'm afraid of. What if I'm not ready to commit? I don't want to hurt him and I don't know if I'm ready for that move yet. I don't want him to hurt me. I've never given my heart to a man and I've never been faithful to a man but, girl, no man has ever treated me like Justin treats me."

"Justin is head-over-heels in love with you, girl, he won't hurt you just as long as you don't hurt him. I know you can be faithful, you just need the right man that can make you settle down."

"So, do you think I should move in with him?" Shyla asked nervously.

"No, I don't think you should. I just wanted to know what your reason was for not wanting to move in with him. The reason I don't think you should is because you two should be married first. If you can move in with him, you can marry him. I think you should open up to him also. Tell him all of your concerns. You've been doing great with being with only him lately, you don't even give any other men the time of day. That shows me that you really love Justin and that you are really happy with him. Tell him you want to take things slow and you want to be married before you move in with anyone. You two remind me of us, me and Terrance, when we first got together."

"Oh no, don't compare us to y'all raggedy shit!" Shyla laughed hysterically as I gave her the most sarcastic look I could create.

"Whatever, Shyla, you are not funny! When do you think you will be ready? Why are you so afraid of commitment? Honestly, girl, tell me."

There was an awkward silence and Shyla wiped the tear that finally managed to escape from one of her eyes. She held her head down and I must admit I had never seen her in that light before. She looked like a scared little girl. This was the first time we actually talked about her behavior and why she never wanted to commit to one man. I hoped she would break it down for me and make me understand why it was she did the things she did. After a long pause, Shyla began to speak.

"Raven, I've never told anyone this so please don't ever repeat this. When I was a little girl, I loved my father. There were three of us, me, Johnny and Pooh. I was daddy's little girl or so I thought. You know him and my mother divorced when I was too young to remember but he would always come and bring us gifts. He always showed a little more favoritism to me, girl, you know I loved that. He'd give Johnny and Pooh five dollars and reach down and slide me six. He was the only important man in my life, all I've ever known. There were times when he'd tell my mother he only wanted to take me with him for the weekend since I was the only girl. I looked up to that man, girl. When I was eight years old he promised me that he would take me to the amusement park, just me and him. When he picked me up he said he wanted to go to his house first. When we got inside his apartment he started playing around with me and tickling me. I was having fun because this was my daddy. Suddenly, he stopped and started rubbing my chest. He said he wanted to see if my breasts were growing like they're supposed to. I allowed him because he was my daddy and I thought he was making sure I was growing properly," she cleared her throat and continued.

"He started unzipping my pants so I grabbed his hand and asked him what he was doing. He said he wanted to give me a check-up. When he took my pants off he started touching me. I felt tears coming down my face because I knew it was wrong. He told me he was going to show me what men and women do when they love each other and he loved me very much. Raven, he raped me. Afterwards I laid in a fetal position crying and he stroked my hair telling me that I should never tell anyone about this or they would put me in a foster home. I was eight years old, I believed him, Raven." Shyla cleared her throat a little more and took a drink of coffee.

"Oh my God, Shyla, I'm so sorry!" I felt my eyes start to water.

"After that day my father would pick me up every other weekend and take me back to his place to have sex. It ruined my whole understanding of what love was and I thought sex equaled love. I had a warped brainwashed mind as he continued to put all types of explanations why he was having sex with me in my head. This went on for three years until one day I got in a huge argument with my brother because he was jealous that dad was spending more time with me than with him and our little brother. I started crying and told him that I would rather him spend time with them and not me because all he wanted to do was have sex with me. My brother's mouth dropped in disbelief and he plopped down on the bed staring at me. I told him how it started when I was eight years old and I even tried to justify it using the explanations dad gave me. My brother just hugged me and then told my mother. My dad was arrested and sentenced to ten years in prison. From that..." Shyla stopped talking when the phone rang. It was someone with the wrong number, I hung up, aggravated that we were interrupted, and edged her to go on. I wanted her to continue.

"Well, from that moment on I started becoming promiscuous. I confused sex with love. I developed a sexual addiction and started craving any type of intimacy. I didn't care if the man didn't want anything else with me or didn't respect me; I just needed to feel a touch from a man. I had to have it or it would feel like I was going through withdrawals. Sex became a drug for me and it was the only way I thought I could feel love. Once the high was gone from one person, I needed to get it from another one. But the bad part about it was I knew that I was slowly dying on the inside. I knew that true love was really all I needed to heal my pain but I didn't know how to go about it. So I found myself having a lot of broken love affairs and the few people I tried to get in a relationship with always ended up being wounded souls who I could relate to. Two wounded souls is a recipe for disaster and that's how it always ended. Since then I've gone through counseling and I learned how to tame myself and the medication I take helps with my depression. But Raven, what if Justin really does love me and I relapse? I'm so afraid of hurting him."

"You won't, Shyla, I will be here helping you through this." Shyla wiped the tears spilling from her eyes as I dashed over and hugged her. I couldn't imagine being raped, especially not by my own father.

When I met Shyla she had just turned fifteen and I was fourteen. I thought she was weird because she wore all black all of the time with dark lipstick and never really smiled. No one really talked to her except for the boys who seemed to fall at her knees and she always gave them the cold shoulder when I saw her. She was always lashing out at the teachers and getting into fights. I walked up to her one day and told her she must love trouble because she's always in it. She looked at me like I was crazy and said "what's it to you?" I went on to tell her how I was tired of having my studies interrupted by the teacher having to stop in the middle of class to say something to her. I told her she was way too beautiful to act so tough. And for the first time I saw her smile. She responded "you think I'm beautiful?" and believe it or not that's how we got to talking.

She told me the reason she acted so tough in class was because she didn't like the way the teacher taught the class. She felt she didn't take time to explain things so that she could understand. I offered to give her tutoring to help her and we've been friends ever since. She told me later in that school year that she pretty much slept with all the guys she gave cold shoulders to. I was surprised but I thought she was just very sexual and I was intrigued by her stories.

"Shyla, I would've never thought you were such a depressed child and that you had to go through all of that. I'm here for you, girl, please don't hold back anything like that from me anymore. I want us to be able to talk about anything! We've been best friends for a long time and all I've ever known about your father is that he died of cancer. You can't be holding out on things like that girl. I could've helped you get over that burden you carried all this time."

"Sorry, Raven, but that was a burden I had to get rid of myself. I am still suffering from it but I have healed considerably. Hold up, I need to go wipe my face."

When Shyla got up from the table and headed to the bathroom I just sat there in disbelief. There was so much about her I thought I knew but I never really analyzed why she abused her body the way she did. I had always been wise enough to know that everything stems from something and mostly it stems from childhood. Our behaviors, our fears and our triumphs all come from the roots and growth development of our childhood. I felt bad for her, all this time she was reaching out for love and no one knew. All this time she was trying to fill a void in her life, becoming promiscuous and nonchalant about her life, and everyone just labeled her as a whore. For the first time since I'd known Shyla, her actions were starting to make sense to me. She came back to the table with her face dried and tried to change the subject.

"So, what are you wearing tonight?" I looked at her and could tell that she was done telling me about her emotional scars so I obliged her subject change.

"I don't know! Let's go pick out something." Shyla followed me to the bedroom trying to force out a smile. My room looked as if a hurricane hit it. Clothes, papers and trash were everywhere but I didn't want to worry about that at the moment because I had a date to prepare for. It was my first date in three years, I was sweating bullets.

"Raven, don't you get to that man's house and start talking about Terrance and Jesus the whole time." Shyla started picking up some of my clothes that fell off the hangers in my closet when Terrance was packing his things.

"No, I can't talk about Terrance. I haven't told him I was married, my name is Debra, remember? And I will talk about God when the opportunity presents itself!" Shyla dropped the pink blouse in her hand and looked at me like she just seen a ghost.

"What? Raven, you haven't told him your real name? I thought you would have told him last night when you called him. Are you going to tell that man your true identity? What if y'all hit it off and then he finds out everything you told him was a lie? You better tell him girl."

"I can't. What if Terrance and I get back together? He can't find out I dated someone behind his back. I don't want Tony to know anything about me, that way I can stay on the low and won't have to worry about Terrance knowing. This is such a small world and I don't want to set myself up like that. I know it's wrong to deceive someone but…" before I could finish Shyla was cutting me off.

"But nothing! That's just wrong. Why do you even want to get back with Terrance in the first place? I know he's your husband, Raven, and even if you two do get back together, Lord forbid, that's fine and dandy, but right now you should be angry with him and ready to go out and do to him what he's done to you. You're acting like you owe this man something- you don't owe him a damn thing!" I plopped down on my bed and just listened to her lecture me as she pointed her finger in my face from time-to-time to get her point across.

"Now you know if you were single and you met some guy you were really digging on and you dated him for a few days and then found out everything he told you about himself was a lie, including his name, then you would be angry as hell, wouldn't you?" she pointed out.

"Yes, I would and even though I hate to say this, you're right. You're right but I will continue to be wrong. There's nothing you can say that can make me change my mind, I can't tell this man who I am. I will have to suffer the consequences if Terrance and I don't get back together and I end up falling for Tony. I am woman enough to know that I will have to eventually make a decision about my marriage, so you don't have to keep reminding me. Regardless if you like Terrance or not, he is my husband and I do not want to get a divorce. I don't believe in divorces and if we can work things out then I will definitely work it out." Shyla just shook her head as I went on.

"And another thing, missy, this may be the first and last date Tony and I have so why should I care about telling him anything about me? He's probably one of those egotistical arrogant pigs who only think about one thing and will do and say anything out of his mouth to get it. Why should I sacrifice my marriage for someone like that? Just help me find something to wear before I cancel this whole thing." I started to get irritated thinking about how men could be. Terrance started getting an arrogant attitude this past year and that's when I noticed the change in his behavior. I never thought my marriage would be on the rocks in only two years. I must've had a defeated look on my face because Shyla just stopped roaming through my closet and stared at me.

"Raven, are you ok?" she looked concerned as she walked over and sat next to me on the bed. I tried to hold back my tears but they started to flow like a river and Shyla reached over and held me as I sobbed away my marriage. I was just waiting for Shyla to say some sarcastic statement like "why are you crying? You are such a fool to cry over him" but she didn't say that. She ran her fingers through my hair and simply told me to let it all out. She let me know she was there for me and to cry all I wanted. I felt this unbelievable bond with her at that moment, I couldn't explain it. I cried for a good five minutes before I heard the door open. Shyla and I looked at each other in a panic as she hurried and wiped my tears.

"Don't let him see you cry." I ran in the bathroom, dried my face and straightened my hair when I overheard the conversation coming from the bedroom.

"Shyla, what are you doing here?"

"Shit, I was about to ask you the same thing. I thought you were told to leave," she snapped back.

"I don't see how it is any of your business what I was told or what I decided to do on my own. Where's Raven?" I could tell he was getting irritated talking to Shyla.

"She's out looking for a real man." On that note I ran out of the bathroom. I couldn't believe Shyla said that, although deep inside I laughed at her sarcasm.

"May I help you, Terrance?" I could barely look him in the face because he looked fine as hell. I felt my hands shaking in suspense of what else would come out of his mouth.

"Uh, can we have some privacy, please?" He gave Shyla the nastiest look as he stared her down waiting for her to leave.

"Shyla, please wait for me in the living room. I will be out very soon." She shook her head as she walked out. Terrance followed to close the door behind her and turned and looked at me. He just stared at me for a moment and sat on the bed. I didn't say anything; my heart was racing as I wondered what he was going to say.

"Terrance, I have things to do. How may I help you?" I sounded like I could care less about him, the Lord knew I wished I could just hold him but that was out of the question.

"Raven, I love you, and I'm sorry. I've learned from my mistakes, please give me another chance. I know you wanted me to leave and I left as you requested but I don't want this to be the end of us. I want you to try to find it in your heart to forgive me." *Forgive him?* Forgive him for sleeping around on me and lying to me? The nerve of him! I know the church talks about forgiveness but I never thought it would be so hard when you're trying to forgive with a broken heart.

"Look, I think we should spend some time away from each other for a while and in that time I don't want to hear from you or see you, unless, of course, there is an emergency. I am very hurt, very hurt, Terrance. I have been nothing but good to you. Not once have you ever had to wonder where I was or ever had to deal with another man. I have been completely faithful to you, Terrance, and all you did was mistreat me, lie to me and cheat on me. I may be able to forgive you but it will take time and you better believe I won't forget." He held his head down while I spoke. This felt good, I was finally able to vent to him and make him actually listen to me. I continued on, walking a little closer toward him.

"You act like I'm an ugly duckling, like I can't find someone else. Do you know how many guys try to holla at me? But I was so proud to say I was happily married and here I am telling these guys *no* when you are running around here telling these women *yes*. I am a strong black woman, Terrance. I was doing good before you and I'll be doing good after you." Man, I was laying it on thick! I was almost convincing myself that I was over him but I was nowhere near that.

"Raven, I'm sorry. I'm so sorry." He broke down and cried. A part of me wanted to run over and grab him and let him cry in my arms but that part of me was crushed and hurt by this man I called my husband. So I stood there saying nothing and tried to keep my composure.

"Raven, baby, please forgive me. Let's work this out. Can I take you to dinner tonight so we can discuss this like adults?" I looked at him in a harsh manner.

"*Adults?* There's only one adult in this room, Terrance, and it ain't you! I can't go to dinner tonight, I have plans." Terrance jumped up off the bed and got in my face.

"Plans with who – that stank ass bitch Shyla?" His nostrils were flaring as I could see his anger starting up.

"First of all, Terrance, Shyla is my best friend and she's not a bitch. Second, it's none of your business who I have plans with but just to let you know, it's not with her. Third, get the hell out of my house because I don't want to see your face any longer." I started shaking again and tears ran down my face. Terrance stared me in the eye for a minute in disbelief right before he turned around and stormed out. On his way out of the room he looked back at me and said in the evilest voice, "fuck you!" The nerve of that man! How was he mad at me? He's acting like I was wrong for being mad at him or wrong for being hurt. Like I'm supposed to shrug my shoulders at the hoes he's been with and just take him back with open arms. I wanted him back but he would definitely have to work for it. I had forgotten Shyla was in the other room when she burst in yelling.

"Girl, you ok?" I wiped the tears from my face, I was fine. I felt stronger than ever because I finally stood up to him. I felt in control. *Now only if I could be in control when I see Tony tonight!* We picked out this black tight-fitting shirt with a very low cut front that showed my cleavage, along with these really tight-fitting pants that flared out at the bottom. Shyla felt I should show off my figure, yet look comfortable since we would be at Tony's house as opposed to a restaurant. She wanted me to let my hair hang since my hair was pinned up when I first saw him and he didn't get a chance to see how long my hair was. Once again, I agreed with her. She had a high fashion sense and she'd never steered me wrong. She gave me the rundown on how to be seductive and how I should fling my hair to one side every time he told a joke.

"Girl, you are so crazy! I'm just going to eat dinner and get to know him. I'm just hoping he can take my mind off of my issues. I'm not trying to flirt with him or do anything else with him." I proclaimed.

"Yeah, yeah, yeah. Just have fun and don't go talking about Jesus *all night* either! You will scare the poor man away."

"Speaking of Jesus, are you going to church with me this Sunday?"

"I'll let you know, Raven," shaking her head.

Tony gave me directions and I was surprised he lived only ten minutes away from me. I made sure I gave his name, address and phone numbers to Shyla in case anything happened to me. Shyla was having dinner with Justin and left my house a few hours prior to my date to go get ready for her own date. I sat on my couch all dressed up, nervously staring at the clock. I had no idea what would happen, so I tried to prepare myself.

Chapter Eleven

TONY: THE DATE

I wanted to call Ray and tell him about the letter I received but I decided to let all that go until after my date. Tonight I wanted to focus on Debra and getting her into bed. This was the first time in a long time that I cooked for a woman in hopes of romance and the first time I was actually a little nervous. I was afraid I might start perspiring again or that the bags under my eyes might return. I didn't want to ruin our evening by getting sick but I felt fine at the moment and looked good too. I shaved my head and left a neat looking goatee on my face. I decided to wear my white button down shirt and some beige khaki pants. That was the outfit that always turned heads whenever I wore it. I looked at the clock: 7:45 P.M. The lasagna was ready and so was I. When I heard my home phone ring I just knew it was Debra canceling.

"Hello?" I answered frustrated by the thought of a canceled evening.

"Tony?" A familiar woman's voice spoke my name although I couldn't quite catch who she was.

"Yes, may I help you?"

"Tony, it's me, Earlene." I was shocked and speechless. I wondered how she got my number. There was an awkward silence on both ends of the phone. I didn't know what to say.

"I'm sorry to call you like this. You should've received my letter by now and I wanted to talk about it more with you." Before she could finish there was a knock at the door. I cut her off and told her to hold on.

I opened the door to a beautiful woman standing there in a black shirt and some tight-fitting jeans that hugged her every curve. A big kool-aid smile came across my face as I greeted her.

"Hello Debra, I was afraid you wouldn't make it." I invited her in.

"Why would you think an awful thing like that? It's 7:55 P.M., I'm right on time." She sat down on the couch as she rubbed her hands together nervously.

"Please excuse me for one minute." I ran to the bedroom and picked up the phone.

"Earlene, you caught me at a bad time. I have important company over and I have to go. I would love to talk to you more about all of this tomorrow. What's your phone number?" She hesitated for a second before she gave me her number. I wrote it down hastily and ran back in the living room with Debra.

"I'm sorry about that. Would you like something to drink?" She made my heart beat rapidly and I just couldn't explain why.

"Yes, what do you have?" Her eyes lit up as I brought out the glasses and the bottle of champagne and placed it on the table with the candles. She had the prettiest smile I'd ever seen and I felt as if I'd known her all my life.

"So, what are we ordering because I'm starving?" She rubbed her flat stomach back and forth while she talked.

"You are beautiful!" I was blown away by her beauty.

"Thank you, but where did that come from?" she asked.

"I am good for saying how I feel. But to answer your question, we aren't ordering anything. I cooked for you, so come have a seat."

"Oh my, you cooked? I feel so special." On her way to the table she stopped to look at the picture on my shelf.

"Who's he?" The picture was of me and Ray on Easter. He had on a stunning blue suit and I had on a black one. We were both very handsome that day and no one could tell us any different.

"That's my brother, Ray. Do you think he's better looking than I am?" She looked me up and down and smiled.

"Naw, I don't go for men with braids. I think you will do." She winked and sat at the table. I lit the candles and brought out our plates. I could tell she was impressed with my set up, *extra points for me.* I poured the champagne and sat down next to her.

"This is great, Tony." She blushed from ear to ear. We started talking and I told her about my job and all the unique people I worked with and she seemed impressed by the diversity of my employees. Right before she started to eat she excused herself to the bathroom as I sat there thanking God for sending me this woman. When she came back she looked at me seriously.

"So, how come you don't have a girlfriend? What's your story? Wait, let me guess. You just haven't found the right woman yet, right?" She looked at me in disbelief as if she didn't believe that a guy like me could not be involved. I cleared my throat, being that it felt a little scratchy, and gave her a *let me explain* look.

"Well, that's partly the answer but to give you the other part, I have not found *you*!" Yeah, that gave me some points as well because her head went down as if she was blushing but trying to hide it. She took a taste of the food and looked like she was having an orgasm. She loved the lasagna and told me over and over again how delicious it was.

"How old are you?" she asked.

"How old do I look?" She looked closely at me. She looked to be no more than twenty-two years old and I wondered if she thought the same about me. Her first guess was twenty-five.

"Wrong, I'm twenty-eight. How 'bout you?" To my surprise we were the same age, I would've never guessed. For some reason I felt extremely comfortable with this woman. The conversation flowed easily and for the first time in a long time I didn't mind talking about myself to a woman I was interested in. I didn't hold back any information.

"I know I asked you this briefly the night we met and I won't turn our conversation into a religious one, but I wanted to ask you again. Do you know Jesus?" She waited patiently for an answer. I didn't want to think about Jesus with what I had in mind for her and for our future, but I knew she wanted an answer.

"As I told you before, I know of Him but I have a lot more to learn. However, He's always been my main man and he's always looking out for me." She smiled at that answer and continued on.

"So, how do you like being a manager?" she inquired.

"I love it. I love having people report to me and listen to my every word." She laughed the most beautiful laugh I'd ever heard and I could see myself hearing that laugh for the rest of my life. I had been doing most of the talking and answering questions so I cut her laughter off and asked her a question I'd been wondering about since I first laid eyes on her.

"So, how come you don't have a man? Wait, let me guess. You're too beautiful and it's hard to find someone who's not intimidated by your beauty. Am I right?" She didn't look at me when I spoke. She continued to eat her lasagna and after a few seconds she looked at me and changed the subject.

"Tony, tell me a little about your personal life, where did you grow up and how many brothers and sisters do you have?" I noticed the subject change but once again, I spoke freely about myself to her. It seemed like I told her my whole life story. I told her how my mother died while giving birth to me and how Ray was my best friend. I told her about Ray's plan to get married and how he was also planning to visit me the following weekend. I talked and talked until I noticed that I had been the only one talking for a whole hour, not counting her occasional "really?" and frequent laughs. She really hadn't told me much at all about herself except for the fact that she was a receptionist at the hotel down the street and that she had been a poet all her life. I stared into her dark brown eyes. *Why had she changed the subject so fast when I asked why she didn't have a man?* She interrupted my thoughts when she asked, "so, what happened next?" I didn't say anything. I just sipped on my champagne and pretended I didn't hear her. After about twenty seconds she cleared her throat as if to let me know that she was still there.

"Hello, did you not hear me? What happened after you found out your aunt was getting a divorce?" she looked a little annoyed.

"Well, I assumed you didn't hear my question an hour ago when you changed the subject so I failed to hear your question, beautiful. I will answer yours once you answer mine. How come you don't have a man?" Once again she put her head down and then looked into my eyes with this sincere look.

"Tony, I don't have a man because I have come to realize that there are no good men out here. I realized that you can give a man your all and they will just take it and run with it. They are never happy with what they have and always looking for more. They are weak, simple-minded creatures that live their lives thinking with the head between their legs as opposed to the head between their ears. Men are just pathetic. You can have a good woman, pretty, cook, clean and take care of your lazy pathetic tail and then you turn around and screw the first pretty girl who shows interest in you. You throw away everything you worked hard to get just for a roll in the hay with someone you barely know, and with a white woman to make it even worse! That other woman only can offer you sex, however, she will try to convince you that she's better than the woman you are supposed to be committed to. You men soak it up because all you're thinking about is screwing her so you start pointing out things she does differently than your woman so you can justify your cheating. Men make me sick!" She got up from the table and sat on the couch. I sat there stunned. It was obvious this woman had been hurt and from the looks of it, she was still hurting. Maybe that wasn't such a great question to ask her. I slowly got up from the table and sat next to her on the couch. She looked at me with tears in her eyes.

"Tony, I'm sorry. Please forgive me." I grabbed her hand.

"It's ok. I guess you are still hurting from your past. I want to be your future. Yes, men are weak at times but we can be strong as well. We can be faithful if we really and truly want to. If we, eventually, felt in our hearts that we were tired of the games and had a woman who felt the same way, then we would also set in our minds that no pretty face, fine body and pretty smile would ever come between the two of them. Something I am learning myself is the fact that you can't hold other people accountable for what someone else has done to you. I was hurt at a young age by a girl I was with and set in my mind that I would hurt women before they hurt me. That attitude appeared to be working for me, Debra, but I always wondered why some nights I went to bed feeling depressed because I didn't have a special woman I could turn to every night and hold." I couldn't believe I was sitting there telling this woman my deepest emotions and thoughts. She gave me her full attention and I could tell she was completely in tuned to what I was saying.

"Well, why do you think it's so hard to just stop hurting women if that makes you depressed after you do it?"

"Well, I don't know. I think there's an image, maybe, I created for myself that makes me accustomed to not having someone special in my life."

"Well, Tony, you are a very handsome man. I'm sure there are a lot of women who would love to be with you and be good to you. Plus you cook too, that's always a great thing. Maybe you just don't give women a chance."

"Yes, I think that's what it is. There are plenty of beautiful women I've met and I wouldn't even attempt to engage in deep conversation with them. I don't allow them to get close to me. Tonight is the first time I've ever told anyone how I truly feel about relationships. I've been in relationships before and they've always ended over some foolishness and not once had I admitted to them that I was just afraid of getting hurt. I know there are some good women out there but I have always convinced myself otherwise." Debra looked very concerned as she rubbed her hand across my cheek.

"Tony, I understand how you feel. I have been hurt and I know that there are good men out there as well, no matter what I say. I know that I am a good woman and I will find a good man. My heart is just breaking right now and I do apologize if I came off wrong earlier. I don't know if I'm ready, right now, to give my heart to anyone else."

"Well, if you don't mind me asking, what happened?"

"Just a boyfriend I had a few months ago. I found out he was cheating on me with a white woman. But if he was cheating on me with a black woman or any other race it still wouldn't matter, cheating is cheating. I haven't had true intimacy in so long. I can't even remember the last time we cuddled and just held each other. This is the first date I've been on since we broke up and I am so afraid I'll say the wrong things to you."

"Baby, nothing you say to me would be wrong except you don't want to see me anymore. That man was a fool to cheat on you, however, I can relate to him and to you. I do know what it's like to be the man that cheats and hurt a good woman. I won't tell you I've never done that because I have. I won't lie to you." Debra moved her hand away from mine when I said that. She looked nervous and put her head down. I grabbed her hand back and continued.

"I want you to know that I am willing to try. Since you are hurting and I am hurting deep inside then maybe we can take this one day at a time. Maybe we are what each other needs. I don't know, what do you think?

"I don't know, Tony, I don't want to hurt you. My life is complicated right now and it's hard to bring someone else into this mess I call my life. There's so much about me you don't know."

"I will find out sooner or later. What I do know is how beautiful you are and how much I want to kiss you." I leaned over and kissed her. It wasn't a normal kiss like I'd given to the other girls I'd met. It was a deep passionate kiss that I'd never experienced before. My temperature rose as I laid her down, still kissing her. My body was on top of her and I could feel her breasts on my chest. I ran my hand across her breasts as I continued to kiss her deeply. When I started to lift her shirt up she grabbed my hand and stopped me. We stared in each other's eyes heavily as I wondered why she stopped.

"Tony, I don't know if I can do this."

"You can do this, Debra, do you want me?" she licked her lips and moaned.

"Uh, yes, Tony. I want you. I really want you." I started kissing her again and raised her shirt to expose her breasts. She wasn't wearing a bra and her breasts were very round and perky. Her nipples were throbbing by now and I wrapped my tongue around them. She moaned in pleasure as I massaged her breasts with my tongue. She reached over my head and took her shirt completely off while I unbuttoned her pants. My manhood was about to explode just at the thought of seeing her naked and I could feel semen soak through my boxers. Once I got her pants off I admired the red silk thongs she wore. I took the thongs off with my mouth and slid them down her legs. When I got them to her feet I took them off the rest of the way with my hands and started to suck on her toes. She moaned in ecstasy as I worked my way up her entire body.

"Oh yes, Tony, don't stop. Yes!" She seemed to be enjoying what I was doing to her. I jumped up, anxious to get in her as I pulled off my shirt. She sat up and started to unbutton my pants and waited for me to make love to her. Just when I was about to stick it in she stopped me again.

"Tony, wait! Do you have a condom?"

A condom? Gosh I hated those things. I wanted to feel all of her so I was a little disappointed. *Should I lie and say I didn't have any?* I thought about it but I figured if I did then she may say we couldn't do it at all so I jumped up and found the box I took from Uncle Steve and threw one on. We made love all night, yes, I said *made love* all night. We did it three times before we were both worn out and when I pulled out that last time, I reached to remove the condom but it wasn't there.

"What's wrong?" she inquired.

"Uh, the condom must've come off."

"What do you mean it must've come off?" she said frantically.

She jumped up looking around the bed for it. I already knew it must've slipped off inside of her but I assisted her in the search. She threw all the covers off the bed and I watched her as she looked under the bed. When she couldn't find it, she just sat there on the floor shaking her head.

"Oh no, what if I get pregnant?" she was close to tears.

I stared at her for a second and grabbed her hand pulling her off the floor. As she sat next to me on the bed, I looked at her and could see the frantic fear in her eyes.

"Don't worry, I didn't get a chance to finish. I stopped before I could release any sperm." I lied. She sighed a sigh of relief and I wrapped my arms around her and laid back on the pillow. I felt bad for lying to her but I didn't want to ruin the evening. I looked at her lying in my arms and felt a peace come over me. Finally, I passed out from exhaustion.

I slept well that night, like a baby. When I woke up I looked at the alarm clock; it was 9:30 in the morning. *Shit!* I was late for work. I turned over to reach for Debra but she wasn't there. I figured she went to the bathroom or out in the kitchen making breakfast. I smiled as I thought about the night I had, it was wonderful.

"Debra!" I yelled. There was no response so I got out of bed and walked into the living room. There was dead silence.

"Debra!" Still there was no answer. I assumed she had left for work and just didn't want to wake me, what a sweetheart. I was sleeping very hard, it's possible she could've tried to wake me but I was just too out of it. Just as I was smiling thinking of our night, I noticed a note lying on the couch. My heart started beating fast as I wondered what it could possibly say. I sat on the couch, looked around to see if there was anything out of place for some reason, and read the note. It read:

"My dearest Tony, this night should've never happened. I'm sorry, Debra"

What did she mean 'this night never should've happened?' It was one of the best nights of my life. I felt a connection with that woman; she was a woman I felt I could at least try to be faithful to. And she wrote 'this night' as if she wrote the note last night as opposed to the morning. She left me in the middle of the night and I felt like a whore. I felt the same way I usually left women feeling after we had sex, sort of like 'wham bam, thank you ma'am.' What was happening? I couldn't go to work with this feeling of abandonment. I was supposed to be there at 8:00 A.M. and it was going on 9:40 A.M. I ran to the phone and there were two messages on the machine. I must've slept hard because I didn't even hear the phone ring.

I played the messages back, hoping it was Debra but it wasn't. Both messages were from my boss wondering where I was. I returned the call and told her I wasn't feeling well, which wasn't an understatement because my body felt drained and unusually tired. I sat there in the nude with the note in my hand and in disbelief. I had to find her and tell her how much of an impact she'd made on me. I wanted to tell her that I'd never felt so open with a woman as to tell her my deepest thoughts and dreams. I told her all about my life, about my mother and about my fears. How could she just walk out on me? I felt a sadness come over me. Had I been leaving women in the middle of the night and making them feel like I felt? Had I been so uncaring about their feelings that they spilled their guts out to me and I just ignored it as if it meant nothing? Had I been so cold?

I took a piss and laid across my bed, I knew how it felt to be left and I was sorry. I had to think of what I was going to do. What if she never called me again? I didn't have her numbers, how could I reach her? Just when I was about to give up on ever finding her again, I remembered she told me she worked down the street at the hotel. *That's it!* I would go to her job and confess my love for her. I got in the shower and rehearsed what I was going to say, "Debra, I love you!" No, that wouldn't work. She would think I was crazy talking about I love her after knowing her for only a few days. "Debra, you did something to me, I just can't explain it. You have changed me!" No good. I needed the perfect words that would at least make her give me a chance. I got in my car and drove down the street to the only hotel on the corner. I remembered Monica talking about the hotel the night we went out. The C-Lake Inn was a popular hotel for college students coming into town. They offered college packages and were known for hosting a lot of the college parties. I walked in and looked around for a receptionist desk. When I got to the front desk, I asked where the receptionist would be sitting and they pointed over to a desk where an elderly woman sat talking on the phone. I stood in front of the woman, waiting impatiently.

"Thank you for calling, sir, I will transfer you over to room service." She hung up and smiled at me with her coffee-stained dentures. She was a pale woman with her snow white hair pinned up in a bun. She looked me up and down before she spoke.

"Yes, how may I help you?"

"Yes, I'm looking for Debra Williams. Where can I find her?"

"Debra Williams? Do you know what room she's in?" She started roaming through her log book.

"Ma'am, she works here. She's a receptionist." The woman closed her book and looked at me in a confused manner.

"Sir, there is no one by that name working here." I figured she was just old and didn't really know everyone who worked there so I gave her a frustrated look.

"Could you check? Maybe she works here when you are off."

"I am the only receptionist here, honey. I've been here for eight years. The only people who cover for me are John and Candy. I'm sorry, sir, I wish I could help you. Hell, I wish you were looking for me but I'm afraid I'm too old for you. You *are* a fine piece of meat." She looked me up and down again and licked her old crusty lips.

"Thank you ma'am," I mumbled. I walked outside the hotel and just stood there. I couldn't believe what I was hearing. Why would she lie to me about where she worked? Who was Debra Williams, really?

Chapter Twelve

RAVEN: THE FREE WORLD

I arrived in front of Tony's apartments at 7:45 P.M. and just sat in the car. I didn't want to be too early out of fear he may have thought I was anxious. I smiled at the thought of him staying in the same apartments I once dreamed of living in before Terrance and I got our house. They were beautiful inside and out but Terrance refused to move into yet another apartment. I wished we could've enjoyed the house bought by creating sweet memories instead of the memories that were now engraved in mind. I couldn't believe I was about to be on my first date in three years, with a *fine* man at that! I just wanted to get back at Terrance for all the times he gave up himself to other women, now it was my turn. I feared backsliding but my heart was so torn that I couldn't focus on that at the moment. I promised myself that I wouldn't talk about Terrance or even think about Terrance once I got up there. I looked at the time: 7:54 P.M., it was time. My heart raced as I walked to his door and knocked.

He opened the door looking so good that I just wanted to jump on him right then and there. He had on this sexy white shirt with only the last two buttons buttoned and some nice khaki pants with some beige sandals... *ooh!* To my surprise he had the table set with candles and the place lingered with the smell of sweet incense. This man had cooked me dinner, I just couldn't believe it. He was a perfect gentleman as he poured my champagne and served me the best lasagna I'd ever tasted. I felt as if I were in heaven until I heard him call me Debra. That reminded me that he knew nothing about me, not even my real name. How could I mislead him this way? I tried to get my deceit out of my mind by asking him a series of questions, all of which he answered with great expertise. He told me all about his childhood and his life as a manager, and surprisingly he worked at the same place I applied to be a trainer at.

"So, where is it you work or do you work?" he asked.

"Uh, I work at the hotel down the street, I'm the receptionist there." I lied. I don't know what made me think of the hotel but that was the first thing that popped into my head. I took a bite of my lasagna and tried to change the subject.

"So, how do you like being a manager?" he seemed to have noticed the change of subject but politely answered my question. As soon as he finished he went back in for the kill with the "how come you don't have a man" question. I had been trying to avoid that question all night by asking him just about everything I could think of about his past relationships, jobs and family affairs. What was I suppose to say *"I don't have a man because I'm married?"* However, the more and more he talked about his lack of ability to commit, the more and more I started thinking about Terrance's lack of ability to commit and I started getting angrier. By the time he asked me that question again I laid it in on him.

"Tony, I don't have a man because I have come to realize there are no good men out there." Tony's eyes got bigger as I went on and on about how men cheat with anything they could get their hands on and not to mention with white women at that. I just couldn't control myself. It felt like I spoke for five minutes straight without taking a breath and was totally embarrassed after shouting "Men make me sick!" I ran to the couch, I was so ashamed of my performance. Terrance had ruined my night once again! It was just too hard to escape the pain he had caused me. I was sure Tony would've told me to leave but instead he came over and comforted me. He shared his hurt from the past with me and offered for us to heal together. Darn, where was this man three years ago? The more he talked, the more I wanted him.

He leaned in to kiss me and the kiss he gave me was a gentle journey to paradise. Terrance had never kissed me that way. My heart raced as I just couldn't believe what was happening. My conscience started in on me as I stopped him a few times but couldn't resist. We made love three times, each time using a new condom. After the third and final time of wild, passionate, hot and steamy sex, Tony laid down in a puddle of sweat and tried to catch his breath. Suddenly he sat up.

"The condom must've come off," he muttered. I almost fainted. This could ruin my life completely. I sat on the floor, about to burst into tears, when he told me he never ejaculated because he saw the condom had come off. *Whew!* Those words were music to my ears as I laid in his arms. Within minutes he was snoring. I started thinking about my deception to Tony and compared it to the deception Terrance gave me and I couldn't believe that I had become just like him. How could God ever forgive me? I couldn't bear to imagine the pain I would inflict upon Tony if I didn't just end it then. When I got up, Tony turned over on his side and didn't skip a beat. I walked into the dining room where dirty plates with lasagna sauce sat on the table and half empty glasses of champagne lingered beside them. I sat in the seat he sat in and smiled. This had truly been a great night. It was one of the most romantic nights I'd experienced in a long time and I didn't want it to end, however, I knew it had to. I looked at my watch: 2:30 A.M. I opened the door to leave but I couldn't, at least not that way. I found a notebook on his table, ripped out a piece of paper and wrote him a note.

"My dearest Tony, this night never should've happened." I placed the note on the couch and walked out. The ride home was a very emotional ride, I cried hysterically as tremendous guilt overwhelmed me. I just cheated on my husband and enjoyed it! Was I as much of a pathetic loser as he was? Was I just a monster out for revenge? I was always trying to get everyone to come to church with me and there I was, a hypocrite myself! I turned my cell phone on after I wiped the tears from my cheeks and saw I had six messages. I pulled the car over to the side to check my voicemail. The first message was from Shyla asking me to give her the details of the date as soon as I got home. The next two messages were hang-ups where I could hear music in the background right before they hung up. The fourth message was Terrance. He simply said "Raven, it's me, call me back." The fifth message was also Terrance and this time he asked where the hell I was, stated he'd been calling me all night and my phone had been turned off. He managed to end that message with an *"I love you."* The last message was Shyla again simply saying I must be having a good time because it was now 2:00 A.M. and she hadn't heard anything from me. She was wondering if

I'd be going to work so we could have lunch. I pulled back on the road and continued home. *How dare Terrance call me questioning me?* What about all the nights I called him and his phone was off? Maybe now he knew how it felt. A sense of satisfaction came over me and I managed to sneak a smile through the dried up tears on my cheek.

I got home close to 3:00 A.M., walked straight to my room and plopped down on my bed. I was exhausted so I set my alarm for 7:00 A.M. and passed out across the bed. I pushed the snooze button on my alarm five times before I managed to crawl out of bed several hours later. I was still tired, mentally and physically, so I just sat there at the edge of the bed staring at the phone. *Should I go in today? Do I really want to be bothered by the stress of my everyday work and the annoying people there?* I sat there thinking of all the pros of going to work. *I'd get to do lunch with Shyla and give her all the juicy details.* That was the only pro I could think of so I picked up the phone and called my manager to let her know that I was still not feeling well and I wouldn't be in again today.

When I got off the phone I crashed back into the bed, pulling the covers over my face. I slept till noon and felt replenished, yet broken. I jumped out of the bed and took a hot shower. I had come to grips, while asleep apparently, that I had the right to live my life because Terrance was living his. The guilt I possessed was for misleading such a wonderful man and for backsliding. I sat on the edge of the tub drenched with water, trying to convince myself that my world was *my* world and I refused, from that moment on, to let anyone come in and disturb *my* world. I knew that I deserved much better than Terrance was giving me. I just hated that I had to resort to the same type of behavior that broke my own heart. I sat there thinking of everything I'd been through within the past year with my marriage, my job and my recent one night affair. I remembered when I was this strong woman, when a man could never drag me down but now I was moping around and acting like my life was over. I missed that strong woman who played no games and took no mess. Right then and there I decided to re-create that woman I once knew. I was tired of moping, tired of being the victim. I wanted to take a stand. Either he goes to counseling with me and to church or I would have to end the marriage.

I immediately got on my knees and asked God to forgive me in my moment of weakness. I asked Him to give me strength to deal with the fact that my marriage may be over. I prayed that He would guide my footsteps from this point forward and help me to make better decisions. When I was done with my praying, I stood up and wiped the steam off the mirror and saw an image of a woman I didn't recognize. It was a woman who I didn't want to be, a woman who gave the old me a bad name. It was a weak and naïve woman who felt she had to fight for a love that didn't love her back. It was a woman who gave in to temptation because of her brokenness and committed adultery herself. I am going to be the woman I once was, happy with or without Terrance. Maybe I needed to be with someone else to help open my eyes. Maybe I needed to know that someone else found me as interesting and beautiful as Terrance once did. But still, that was no excuse to stoop to his level.

If Terrance wanted to run around on me like a nut, then I'd let him. That didn't give me the right to do the same thing. I felt a burst of energy and determination build up inside of me as I rushed to put on some jeans and a tee shirt. I had a plan that generated in my mind and I wanted to put it into action before I changed my mind. I was going to get rid of that Terrance for good unless he agreed to counseling. I stared at the phone, plopped on the bed and took a deep breath. I picked up my home phone and dialed his number as fast as I could.

"Hello, where the hell have you been?" he answered on the first ring.

"Don't worry about where I've been because I wasn't with you. I'm just calling to" before I could finish, he cut me off.

"Why aren't you at work? What's going on? I'm on my way there now, we have to talk."

"No, we don't have anything to talk about, Terrance. I want a divorce." The words rolled out of my mouth so effortlessly that, for an instant, I was shocked by it myself. All the anger and hurt that I felt came back the moment I heard his voice. I wasn't sure if counseling would even work. What if he just told the counselor everything he was expected to say but it wasn't sincere? I refused to be his dummy any longer, I deserved better. There was pure silence on the phone as I waited for a response.

"Hello, did you hear me?" Just as I asked if he heard me, the operator came on the phone "if you'd like to make a call, please hang up and try your call again." He hung up on me and I knew he was on his way to my house, so I grabbed my purse and jumped in the car. I didn't want to see his face or hear his voice any longer; I was too angry and ashamed. I started driving, unaware of where I was heading. I decided to head to the mall, and grabbed my cell phone to call Shyla.

"Raven, I knew you would call off today but what I didn't know is that you wouldn't at least call me on my lunch break to give me the details. How dare you call me now when it's about time for me to go back to work?"

"I'm sorry, I hadn't noticed the time. I will give you all the details, Shyla, but I have mixed emotions about everything. Why don't I stop by your house today after you get off?" I wanted to be far away from my house. As soon as I pulled up into the mall parking lot, my cell phone rang and it was my home number. I let the call go to voicemail and went inside the mall. It was a fairly huge mall and not as crowded as it was on the weekends. I walked straight into the shoe store that I always loved to shop at. There sat the prettiest black high heels I'd ever seen and I just had to have them!

Shopping was great therapy but I knew I really needed to go to church and throw myself on the altar! After I left the mall, I went to get my car detailed so I hung around the waiting room reading magazines until they were done.

"Such a remarkable looking woman!" I heard a voice say. When I looked up to see who owned the sexy deep voice, I was stunned by the handsome man standing in front of me. I suddenly got nervous as I responded.

"Well, thank you for that compliment!" I blushed. He sat down in the chair next to me and leaned over to look at the magazine I had sitting in my lap.

"Well, I was talking about the woman on the cover of the magazine, but you are quite remarkable as well!" I was so embarrassed.

"I'm sorry. I thought you were talking about me." Just as I said that, my car was ready for pick up.

"What do I have to do to take you out to lunch?" I looked at him with surprise, it was going on 1:30 P.M. and I was starving. He was wearing a cream colored shirt with some nice dark jeans. His tennis shoes were a cream and blue mixture and looked like they could've been brand new. He had a sneaky grin on his face and some devious looking eyes that had a slight slant to them. His teeth were pure white and he had these full lips that brought out his smile even more. I thought about it for a second and then remembered that, regardless, I was still a married woman!

"My name is Raven, by the way, what's yours?"

"I'm Flint. It's great to meet you, Raven. So, would you like to have lunch with me? I would really like to get to know you better."

Flint? What kind of name was Flint?

"Well, I'm in a complicated situation right now. Going to lunch with you may not be a good idea but I appreciate the offer. My car is ready now so I will go on my way. Maybe I'll run into you again one day!"

"Well, Miss Raven, I can respect that. Let me give you my number in case things change." He handed me a pizza card with his number hand written on it.

"I'm here with my mother waiting for her to get her car detailed." He whispered."Why are you whispering?" Something just wasn't right about him all of a sudden and I started to think he was a total loser.

"I don't know, I always whisper when I talk about my mother. I guess I'm just so used to her eavesdropping in my room when we're at home. I want..." before he could finish I cut him off.

"You live with your mother?" I looked shocked and annoyed at first but then I tried to relax my face. It's possible he could've had a house getting built and just staying with his mother until it was done. I hadn't planned on calling him anyway but I was just curious at that point.

"Yes, I stay with my mother. Is that a problem?"

"No, not really. How old are you again?" I knew he never told me how old he was, I was just trying to make a sarcastic remark to make it clear to him that grown men should *not* live with their mothers.

"I'm thirty-seven. I'm not working right now so I stay with my mom until I can get me a job, been unemployed for about a year now. It's just really hard finding work without a high school diploma, you know?"

"No, I don't know. Well, good luck with that!" Just as I was about to walk away, I got the urge to tell him about my Jesus!

"I would like to talk to you about Jesus, Flint. I'll be right back." I walked away from him for a few minutes to pay for my detailing. When I came back, Flint was gone. I guess Flint didn't want to hear about Jesus! Devils will always flee!

I left my cell phone in the car and when I grabbed it I noticed the voicemail symbol flashing. I sighed before I punched in my password. I just knew it was Terrance leaving a million messages, but I only had one message and it was from Shyla telling me she was getting off early and to meet her at her place at 2:00 P.M. I was relieved to hear she was off because I really needed someone to talk to. A part of me wanted to call Kathy so she could pray for me, but I didn't want to involve her in my issues. I pulled up to the A-Wing restaurant and ordered something to eat before I headed over to Shyla's place. While I was driving, I suddenly did a U-turn and headed to my church. There were three people in the church sanctuary on their knees praying. I walked down to the altar, broke down crying and dropped to my knees. I cried hysterically for a few minutes before I could even get a prayer out. "Father God, please forgive me! Please guide me. I don't know what to do, Lord. I'm so broken." That's all I kept saying. I couldn't find any other words to say. God knew my heart. I got up after a few minutes and felt a sense of peace come over me.

I started thinking about how much the devil had interfered in my life. I didn't even make it to church last week due to all the foolishness that went on. I pulled up to Shyla's house and she wasn't there yet so I pulled out my journal and wrote down my feelings:

"The Devil himself been hanging out with me,
whispering in my ear reminding me how I used to be.
Been sitting back telling me, "You'll never win!"
Trying to drag me down into a life of sin.
Interfering with the love I have for my house,
Throwin' pieces of salt on me and my spouse.
Trying to convince me there's no hope being saved,
"You'll never be more than you are," in my mind he engraved.
Dressed up forbidden fruit and offered it to me,
"You'll never be happy 'til you take of it...go ahead...eat."
Sitting with me in church, "Do you really believe what that Pastor just said?
If you listen to me I'll be sure to get you ahead."
Shouted out a laugh when I called out to the Lord,
asking me, "Why tithe when you know you can't afford?"

Keeping me confused, not knowing what I want to do,
so I drop to my knees, "Father God, I'm depending on you"
I cried out, "God, the devil is enticing me by raising his voice."
And the Lord responded, "I have given you the discernment of choice.
As long as you believe in me I'll keep you safe in my arms,
when you feel you can't go on, read the 35ᵗʰ Psalms."
I suddenly felt relief as my soul He started caressing,
My child, the Devil himself can't keep you from manifesting!"

I breathed a sigh of relief, leaned my driver's seat back, and listened to the slow jams playing on the radio. I closed my eyes and thought about the first time Terrance and I danced together. We were in a smoky hole-in-the-wall club that we stopped at on our way to New York so I could use the restroom and Terrance came in to order a beer. Just as we were about to leave, this beautiful love song by Whitney Houston came on. Terrance grabbed me and we danced, staring into each other's eyes. It was such a lovely moment that I chose to never forget. It was a moment that I wished would last forever. I felt a tear run down my face just as I heard Shyla blow her horn.

"Hey girl, wake up. Come on, I'm going inside." She was wearing a cream colored business suit and had her hair back in a ponytail. She didn't have on much make-up at all and she looked very professional. Somehow, in that light, she didn't look like the Shyla I used to know. The Shyla I was looking at was a new and improved person who now took life seriously and I smiled at the change.

"You can eat at the table, let me slip into some jeans and I'll be right back. Can't wait to hear all about Tony!" For a slight second I had forgotten about Tony. I had been trying to keep him off of my mind all day and focus on my husband. My body was still tingling from the love making we shared. I felt so bad for lying to him but I knew it was for the best. When Shyla walked back into the room she had on some skintight jeans and a belly shirt that hugged her breasts. She was beautiful, inside and out. She stared heavily into my eyes for a moment without saying a word. It was a very awkward moment and it made me feel a little uncomfortable for a second. I cleared my throat and broke the silence.

"So, girl, how was your day?" I asked as she continued to look me in my eyes while smiling.

"Shyla? Hello, anyone home? What's up with you today, girl?" I was feeling my hands start to sweat.

"My fault, girl, I'm sorry. You just look like you have this glow about you and I was just admiring it. Tell me all about Tony and don't leave out any details."

I told her every detail about our conversation, how I avoided his questions and how I went off on him about men's behaviors. When I got to the part of leaving the note, Shyla just shook her head.

"Why in the hell did you do that?" I didn't answer her question. I continued on about my shopping day and about Flint. She laughed and in the middle of her laugh I cut her off.

"I told Terrance I wanted a divorce." She froze in her laughter.

"Get outta here, you're lying." I shook my head and she took the smirk off her face.

"The moment I heard his voice I became so angry. Our wedding vows were supposed to be sacred and he violated them," I put my head down and uttered, "and so did I."

"You are serious. My Raven's growing up and becoming a big woman. I am so proud of you, and I am here for you. We can get through this, girl, but you gotta be willing to see it through," she looked at me proudly as she continued on.

"You will be a free woman. You can do it, woo hoo!!!!" Shyla stood up on the table and yelled, jumping up and down. "Go Raven!!! Woo hoo!!!"

"Shyla, get down from there. I felt so much guilt for doing to Terrance the very thing he did to me. I don't want either one of us to continue to commit adultery. This is not who I am, I just had a moment of weakness. I pray that God forgives me. I have mixed feelings about everything. Divorce is never the best answer but I will continue to feel hurt if we don't do counseling. Then I think about him hitting me, and if he'll hit me once then more than likely he'll hit me again. And then there are the affairs. I don't know how many other women there have been. I don't know what to do. I really need you to come to church with me this Sunday, Shyla. I need you there for moral support. I am broken and confused."

"Yes, I will be there for moral support. We will get through this together. I just hate to see you so down. I know that you deserve a lot more than what you've been getting from him." Before I knew it, Shyla jumped off the table, leaned in and kissed me on the lips. It was a quick and soft peck that took me off guard. I just stood there as she looked at me. The silence was so loud around us that I couldn't hear a sound. Then she said in almost a whisper, "Raven, welcome to the free world."

I didn't want to be in the free world. I wanted my marriage. I wanted the man I married two years ago. I wanted to be happy. I didn't say a word as she tried to change the subject.

"I have to call Justin. I missed him all day today." Shyla always had a way of changing the subject when things got too deep or awkward. She picked up the phone and called him, and had the biggest smile on her face the entire time. When she got off the phone we sat and talked for hours about Terrance and about how much she was in love with Justin. Justin was due to stop by her house for dinner so I headed home to give them some privacy. I felt a lot better after stopping at the church and talking to Shyla. My faith in God calmed my nerves. I knew that He would give me the strength and wisdom to make the right decisions.

When I got home, Terrance's car was in the driveway. I didn't know if I had the will to argue. The house was quiet as I looked around the house for him. When I got to my bedroom, I saw the door was cracked so I walked in. Terrance was fast asleep on our bed so I sat down next to him and watched him sleep. He looked so peaceful that I wished I could capture that peace forever. I didn't want to wake him, so I gently moved his arm and laid on his chest. *The free world? I just want my husband.*

Chapter Thirteen

TONY: THE METAMORPHOSIS

The day after Debra walked out on me was the longest day of my life. I felt the pain that I had caused others in my life. I never once thought someone could treat me the way I had treated the women I encountered. Maybe I was getting what I deserved. I sat in my window sill and stared out into space. I didn't know what was so special about Debra since I really just met her but I felt as if I knew her all my life. I was almost thirty years old and had never really been true or faithful to a woman. Sometimes I hid behind the relationship Earlene and I had as an excuse for why I was the way that I was. But that only lasted for a short amount of time. The truth was I was afraid of loving too hard. My brother Ray was about to get married and I would love to get married and have a family one day. That lifestyle would be ideal for me but I just couldn't seem to allow myself to open up to a woman, at least not until now. Out of all the women I shacked up with, Debra knew more about me than they would ever know. Why she walked out on me and lied to me about where she worked was beyond me but I felt it was only a matter of time before someone gave me a wake-up call.

I didn't go to work. I just sat there for at least an hour, deep in thought. Before I knew it, I found myself in a puddle of sweat, my clothes were soaked and wet and my throat felt scratchy. There was another big red sore forming on the side of my cheek that was starting to get a little irritated and throbbed a bit. On top of that, I broke out into hives with red bumps all over my body and they itched like hell. I seemed to be getting worse. I could remember getting bit by a spider a few weeks ago and it's possible my symptoms were coming from that bite. I grabbed the phone book to search for a doctor; of course it had to be a woman. All the names sounded like white women but I wanted to find a black woman so I scrolled down the pages until I ran across a black name. Seriah Jones. What a powerful name for a black doctor. I called to make the appointment for later in the day but she couldn't see me until a few days later. I needed to take some kind of medicine to keep me going until then so I jumped in my car and drove down to the corner store.

"Excuse me, sir, can I speak with you for a moment?" I looked up in the aisle to see a young man with a small afro with a part on the side. He was a tall and lanky black man and he held a Bible in his hand.

"Sir, have you given your life to Jesus?" That was a good question. Normally I would have told him to beat it but I somehow took it as a sign. *Was God trying to tell me it was time to wake up? Was He trying to tell me it was time to change my life?*

"No, I have not." I looked down in shame as I responded to his question.

"Well, without Jesus, there is nothing. You must repent for your sins and ask the Lord to come into your heart. Are you a member at a church right now?"

"No, sir."

"Well, here's the address to the church I oversee. My name is Pastor Jihal Johnson. Can I expect to see you this Sunday, my son?" As he wrote down the church address, I explained to him how busy my schedule was but I would make it a point to come visit his church. Just as he was about to leave, he turned around and looked at me.

"Son, are you feeling okay? You're not looking so good. You might want to go see a doctor soon." I guess I was looking a little sickly.

"I must be coming down with something, Pastor. I have an appointment in a few days."

"Well, you make sure you go. God bless you."

When I got home I put the beer I bought in the refrigerator and took two teaspoons of the flu medicine that promised to make me feel like a million bucks. I sat on the edge of my bed and noticed Earlene's number sitting on the nightstand. I stretched out on my bed, grabbed my phone and started to dial. I must've passed out from exhaustion because when I woke up I still had the phone in my hand with a half-dialed number.

It was two in the morning and I couldn't believe I had been asleep all of that time. I sat up for the rest of the night wondering how a woman could sleep with me and then dump me. Stuff like that never happened to me. Maybe that's why I was feeling so much pain from it. I had never been rejected like that. I couldn't get over the fact that she could do that to me, even after I admitted to her how I felt about relationships. I stayed up for three more hours wallowing in my sadness until I nodded off, getting a little more sleep before I went to work.

When I arrived to work Thursday morning, Sheena was waiting for me in my office.

"Tony, are you feeling better? Looks like you've lost weight since last week and you look as though you haven't had any sleep." She looked very concerned.

"I'm fine, Sheena, thanks for asking. My pants are fitting a little loose this morning, perhaps I have lost a few pounds. I lost my appetite over the past few days because this cold is really kicking my butt."

"Well, you really didn't have to come in this morning. There's an important meeting today with the Director of the company, did you forget? You don't seem like you're up to meeting with anyone today."

I had forgotten all about the meeting. I was supposed to go over my expectations for the company and my future goals. It was to be an important meeting that could place me in a position where I would be set for life.

"Sheena, what time was that scheduled for?" I looked through my planner nervously.

"In thirty minutes! I can reschedule for you if you'd like me to. I don't really think you look too presentable, if you don't mind me saying." I looked her up and down. She *never* looked presentable to me and I was insulted that she would say such a thing to me. Before I could respond, she continued.

"Sir, there's a really dark sore on your cheek. What is that?" Just as she said that, I felt my heart start to race. The sore was red and puffy when I woke up and it was quite painful. I brushed past her, saying nothing, and walked quickly to the restroom to the mirror. Before me was a pitiful sight. I had bags under my eyes, which apparently just arrived, and the sore had turned darker. As I stared at myself in the mirror, it did appear that I lost about five pounds in my face and beads of sweat popped up on my forehead. I wasn't really feeling like my normal self and sadness swept over me. The last time I had a cold it never felt like this. *Damn spider must've infected me with something.* I washed my face and tried to get myself together, I couldn't miss that meeting. David was a hard person to catch up with and that was his only free day for the next few months. When I walked out of the restroom, Sheena was standing there with a worried look on her face.

"Are you going to be ok, sir?" I tried not to give her that *leave me the hell alone* look so I cleared my throat and told her I would be fine.

"I'm heading to David's office now. Please let him know that I'm coming."

"Ok, but if you want to go home after the meeting then you can. We can handle things without you."

"That might not be a bad idea. I have a doctor's appointment tomorrow so I probably won't be back in until Monday. I'll talk it over with David as well. I really don't like missing work, especially since I've only been here for such a short period of time."

When I got on the elevator it smelled like someone had bathed in some really loud cologne and I tried to cover my nose as much as I could. When I got off on the top floor where David's office was located, I noticed it looked like a totally different world. There were no cubicles and all the offices were made out of wood furniture. There were large desks and cushioned chairs inside of the offices. I was in awe when I imagined having the biggest office on that floor facing the pond. The receptionist in the front cleared her throat to get my attention as I looked around in amazement.

"Sir, I asked if I could help you?" She was a young looking woman with pretty blue eyes and pitch black hair. She wore a dark blue business suit and had on some bright red lipstick. Her smile was crooked but she seemed like a pleasant person as she smiled heavily at me.

"Yes, ma'am, I'm sorry. I was just thrown off by the beautiful offices up here. I'm here to see David Patten, he's expecting me."

"Oh, you must be Tony Wilkerson, I'm Cindy Shelton. I'm pleased to meet you, follow me." She stood up to shake my hand and I followed her through the maze of offices as all the businessmen stared at me wondering who I was. Some of the nameplates sounded familiar from the newsletters we received from all the corporate big shots. It was good to put faces to those names. I almost forgot how sick I looked until Cindy stopped at David's office and turned around and asked me if I was feeling okay.

"I'm fine, just coming down with a slight cold. Thank you." I walked into David's office and almost forgot how *sweet* he was until he looked me up and down and smiled from ear to ear.

"Tony, it's great to see you. Sheena told me you weren't feeling too good, do you know what's going on with you?" He pointed to the chair for me to have a seat.

"I don't know what it is but it's tearing me up. I have been exhausted and breaking out into sweats. I was bit by a spider a while ago and I think it has something to do with that, on top of a cold. I haven't really been coughing much lately but it may be a combination of the two. I have a doctor appointment tomorrow so hopefully I will be fine after that. I wanted to see if it was ok if I left after we meet and take tomorrow off."

"Of course, you could've rescheduled our meeting as well. What made you come in today?" I'm sure he wanted me to say *"because I wanted to see you,"* but that wouldn't happen.

"Well, David, I have a lot of goals for myself and moving up fast in this company is one of them. I would never want to miss a meeting with someone such as yourself to talk about my future, especially when you're so hard to catch up with." David laughed and seemed to agree with my last statement. For the next hour we talked about me being the manager over the team I was assigned to as opposed to the assistant manager position I was hired for. I was only there for a few weeks and got a promotion already! He explained how the manager had been out for quite some time and they were ready to replace her. We talked about all the corporate big shots and their focus and goals for the company. David impressed me even more when he told me how he started out in the mailroom and moved up in the company in a matter of seven years as a manager and two years later as Director. It was an inspiration to me and I enjoyed listening to him. He was a very educated man with plenty of street smarts and even more business smarts. After a while David stopped his business talk and looked at me with great concern.

"Tony, can I ask you a personal question without you getting offended?" David looked a little worried as he awaited my answer. It always made me nervous when people asked questions like that, usually that meant it *would* be offensive but they just hoped you didn't jump on them.

"Yes, we're both adults. Shoot."

"You don't have to answer this question if you don't want to. What is your sexual preference?" Somehow that question didn't baffle me as much as I thought it would. I was comfortable with my sexuality because I loved women and nothing more.

"I am very straight, and you?" I already knew his answer but I figured it was a matter of *you asked me so I can ask you.*

"I've been gay my whole life. I was just concerned because a friend of mine had a similar sore on his thigh and he…." he cleared his throat and suddenly changed the subject.

"You know what, we can discuss this later. It was nice talking to you, Tony. I'd better get my stuff together, I have another meeting in a few minutes." I was stunned by his sudden change of subject.

"What were you about to say about your friend? He was gay? Well, David, I can honestly tell you that a sore can't dictate whether you're straight or gay. I thought you were an educated man." I tried to place a giggle at the end of that statement in case it offended him but I got a little irritated by his comment. That was like saying if I had the same haircut as a gay guy then that meant I was gay or that the gay guy was straight. I just couldn't understand the reasoning behind his question. I sat in anticipation waiting for his response. He seemed to be quite nervous and I noticed he wouldn't look directly at me.

"I don't know, I lost my train of thought and forgot what I was about to say. It's definitely not my place to say anything about your sore and I do apologize. Tony, I'm concerned about your health and I really would like you to take as much time off as you need. You said your appointment is tomorrow, correct?"

"Yes, it's tomorrow. I don't see what the big deal is. I told you I got bit by a spider."

"No big deal here, I believe that's what happened to my friend as well. Yes, a spider bite! They had to run a lot of tests on him to see if there was any poison released in his body. Tony, make sure they run *all* the tests."

"Your friend was bit by a spider? What are the odds of that? What color was the spider?"

"Tony, I've got to be going. Please go home and get you some rest, I insist." He was rushing me out of the office and his tone and body language became cold and demanding. I didn't know how to take it so I just got up, shook his hand and told him I would see him in a few days. I thought it was weird how the whole chemistry changed when he started talking about his friend. Maybe his friend was hurt badly by the spider, I didn't know. I didn't have time to worry about it, I just wanted to go home and lay down. I thought about Debra's smile the entire drive home and imagined her waiting for me at my doorstep. When I got to the front door there was no one there. I had several messages on my machine but they were from Aunt Tina, Reigene and Ray. None were from Debra.

'Ring' the phone startled me as I found myself dozing off in the living room.

"Hello?"

"Hello, Tony?" It was the voice I had been longing for. It was Debra, my heart raced as I sat up in the recliner.

"Debra? Debra, where have you been?" I asked in anticipation.

"Tony, I'm sorry I left the way I did. Will you forgive me?"

"Yes, of course. I went to your job but they said you never worked there, is that true?" There was silence on the other end of the phone.

"Hello, Debra?"

"Yes, Tony. I'm here. Yes, that's true. I lied to you about where I worked because I didn't know if I would like you."

"Do you?" I asked

"Do I what?"

"Do you like me?"

"Yes, Tony, I like you very much. I haven't been able to stop thinking about you no matter how hard I try."

"That's how I feel. I know we just met each other but Debra I want us to work on trying to be together. What do you think about that?" I waited anxiously for her reply.

"Tony, there's so much about me that you don't know. I wouldn't feel right answering that question until I'm able to open up to you. I need more time."

"I have all the time in the world, Debra. I don't know what it is about you, girl, but you got me walking around here thinking of ways to make myself a better man. I think it's just the calmness of your voice when you speak to me or the sincerity in your eyes when you look at me. It was the comfort I felt when I was next to you, and when I made love to you. Debra, I don't know what it is but I think God is trying to tell me something and for the first time in my life, I'm listening. Don't ever disappear like that on me again, sweetie."

"We will talk soon, Tony."

"I need a number to contact you, can you give me that?" She hesitated for a second and then explained how that wouldn't be a great idea.

"Tony, it was good hearing your voice. I have to go but I'll call you tomorrow, good night."

"Please call me tomorrow. Good night, my love." I hung up the phone, grinning from ear to ear. That night I made a vow to God that if He allowed me to be with Debra, then I would give her my all and treat her like a lady. I vowed that I would find out about her and wait before having sex with her again. I didn't know what it was she was hiding or why I couldn't have her number but I really didn't care. I figured it was that time in my life to have a relationship and I found myself envious of Ray. He was getting married and would have the life I secretly wished for myself, but was too afraid to go out and get. I knew I couldn't change overnight and that it would take work, however, this was the first time I'd even taken the first step to make a change. I was proud of that.

I dragged my feet through my bedroom door and sat on my bed. In the corner of my room was a Bible and it seemed to stare at me. Only God could stop the way I was feeling, no one but Him. I'd never been a real religious man but I'd always kept a Bible close by and anytime I got depressed I would open it up to read the Matthew chapter and recite the words of Jesus.

Tears fell on the pages as I began to pray that the Lord forgive me for all the wrong in my life. It seemed like my world was crumbling around me and I felt a loneliness that I'd never felt before. I felt like I was losing my mind, losing my health and losing the love I had for myself. I prayed and cried all night, even yelling at times for God to come down and renew my strength and my faith and to save my life. There had been plenty of times in my life that I could've gotten saved but I thought that my life would be over if I did. I assumed that all the fun I was having would have to cease, but I often saw groups of saved people out having more fun together than I was. I always made an excuse why I shouldn't give my life to the Lord. I'd say "I still have a few more women to screw," or "I'll do it next year." Once that year came, I always had other reasons why I needed to wait. I knew that if I confessed Jesus Christ is Lord with my mouth and allowed Him into my heart that I would be saved. But I also knew that if I did that, all the foolishness I'd been dealing with in my life would have to stop. I wasn't quite sure I wanted to do that just then, but I think I am ready.

The next morning I got up feeling a little weak so I tried to eat some oatmeal before I headed to the doctor. My appetite was steadily fading so I dumped the oatmeal in the garbage after only a few bites and headed on my way. I sat in the doctor's office for over twenty minutes waiting for them to call my name. I had already filled out the new patient papers and sat there impatiently to see the doctor. I was curious to see how fine Dr. Jones would be so I went to the restroom and made sure I looked presentable. There were slight bags under my eyes. My hives were itching and I felt weak but I managed to drag myself back to the waiting room.

"Mr. Tony Wilkerson."

Finally, I was being called. The nurse took my temperature and weighed me. I had lost ten pounds. She gave me a gown to put on before the doctor came in to see me. I always hated those gowns because it made me feel like a woman. It looked like a dress and on top of that my butt was out. I sat on the bed feeling humiliated when Dr. Jones walked in. She was an awful sight. She was extremely thin with no breasts or butt and had these really huge eyes. Her nose was wide and her nostrils seemed to flare. She asked me about my symptoms and I made sure I mentioned the spider. Her hands were cold as she examined the hives and the sore on my body.

"I'm going to ask you a series of questions, Mr. Wilkerson, and I need you to be completely honest with me. Are you a drug user?"

"Please call me Tony. No, I don't use drugs."

"If you are sexually active, what forms of protection do you use?"

"I know I should always protect myself, doctor, but I've had unprotected sex more than I've had protected sex. I hate the way a condom feels. What does that have to do with my cold and spider bite?" I asked.

"Sir, I'm just trying to gather some information for my files. Are you married, sir?" she continued to write as she asked her questions.

"Please call me Tony! No, I'm not married but I just met this beautiful woman who may be a perfect candidate for it." I grinned at the doctor but she did not crack a smile. Her face was serious as she called the nurses in to take blood tests.

"Doctor, can you just give me some antibiotics so I can get rid of these symptoms? I'm miserable!"

"We must run tests on you, Tony, to see exactly what the issue is. How long have you had that lesion on your face?"

"It's been there for a while but it's starting to get darker. I have one on my chest as well." I showed the doctor.

She looked concerned and stated that she would call me back in a few days once the test results came in. I asked for medication but she refused to give me any until she knew exactly what the problem was. She told me to take over the counter headache medicine when I felt a headache coming on.

When I got home I was exhausted. I must've passed out on my couch without knowing because I slept all day. I woke up at 4:00 A.M. to get a glass of water and went back to sleep. A loud knocking on the door awakened me at 8:34 A.M. and I sat up in my bed startled. When I opened the door, a familiar woman stood there with a child.

"Hello Tony, it's been a long time."

I couldn't believe Earlene was standing at my door. She was still just as beautiful as I remembered her. She wore an expensive looking dress, pearls and heels. A little overdressed for an early Saturday morning outing but it was definitely a sight worth seeing. Her smile was perfect and her eyes sparkled as she stood with her arm around the handsome young boy standing next to her. I was speechless as I stared at the two of them.

"I'm so sorry to just pop up this way. I thought maybe you were upset with me because you rushed me off of the phone and never called me back. I really wanted you to meet Charles and I wanted to talk to you. Did we catch you at a bad time?" She inquired.

"Uhhhh, no, no! Please come in."

There was an awkward silence for a moment as we all sat on the couch. I made small talk with Charles, asking him about his school and what type of sports he liked. Just as we finished that conversation, Earlene chimed in.

"Is there anywhere we can go talk in private?"

I turned the television on for Charles and guided her to my bedroom. Once we got in the room I plopped on the bed, stunned that I had just met my son. She stood there, stared at me for a small moment and then smiled.

"Before you think ill of me, let me explain. I left town when I found out I was pregnant and Kevin came with me. He told me not to get a DNA test because my son was going to be his regardless. We got married and he became a successful lawyer. He even took anger management classes to make sure that he was no longer abusive toward me like he was in high school because he didn't want Charles to grow up that way. We both knew that Charles looked just like you but neither one of us spoke a word of it. We've been in love and married all of this time; we were very happy."

"*Were?* Guess that happiness wore out, huh?" I snarled.

She sat next to me on the bed, rubbed her wedding ring as if to admire it, and held her head down.

"Kevin died a few months ago. He had cancer. On his dying bed he told me that he wrote me a letter but didn't want me to open it until he died. I obeyed. The letter said that he's always known that Charles was not his because he was diagnosed with being sterile at a young age. He said that it was important that I find you and give you an opportunity to get to know Charles if you wanted to. He went on to insist that I never go after you for child support because, even after death, he wanted to be the one supporting us. He left us a large sum of money and a great deal of memories. I miss him so much, Tony."

At that moment Kevin didn't sound like the horrible girl-snatcher that I remembered him to be. He sounded like a sincere father who loved a child that he knew wasn't his. It appeared that he did a great job raising him for the past ten years and wanted to pass the torch to me to carry it on. Charles was the son that he never could have. I had to admire him for his devotion and for his respect for me as his real father.

"Does Charles know that I'm his father?" I inquired.

"Yes, after Kevin died I had a heart to heart with him and explained everything to him. He knows that it wasn't your choice to not be in his life. I was afraid to tell him without really knowing if you wanted to be a part of his life, but I figured either way he should know the truth."

"I do. I do want to be a part of his life. Thank you for letting me know and for giving me a chance. I was angry with you for a long time but lately I've come to realize that I needed to forgive you in order to move on. I need to get my life right."

"That's great to hear. We won't stay long today but maybe we can come back tomorrow." She waited anxiously for my response.

"That's fine. I'm not really feeling well this morning anyway. I'm going to go to church tomorrow. I'd love for you and Charles to come with me."

"We'd love to! I can come pick you up if you want or we can just meet you there."

"My neighbor, Monica, has been going through a lot lately so I wanted to invite her also so I'll probably ride there with her to make sure she comes. I can ride back with you and Charles and maybe the three of us can go grab a bite to eat afterwards." Earlene just smiled and we sat there in silence for what seemed like a lifetime before Charles knocked on the door before opening it.

"Dad, can I have something to drink?" *Dad? Someone was calling me dad.* My heart dropped. That word shocked every cell in my body and it felt surreal. Before I could answer I felt a tear fall down my cheek.

"Yes, son, you can have anything you want."

Chapter Fourteen

RAVEN: RISING ABOVE THE ODDS

Terrance woke up in the middle of the night and started shaking me trying to wake me. The look he had on his face was very innocent looking. We laid there staring at each other before he finally spoke.

"Hi, I fell asleep waiting for you. My work clothes are back at the hotel so I have to go so I can get ready for work in the morning. I think I should stay away for the next few days to give us some time to think and maybe we can get together and talk this weekend. Is that ok?" he waited patiently for an answer.

"Yes, Terrance, that's ok. I don't want to argue anymore. I want us to really listen to each other and talk."

"I agree, I'm tired of arguing. I'll come over Saturday morning."

He smiled and kissed me gently on my forehead before he headed out. I spent the rest of the night tossing and turning. I couldn't seem to get Tony off of my mind, no matter how hard I tried. I had no idea what was going to happen with my marriage but I did know that if I wasn't married then I would definitely be interested in Tony. I tried my best to go back to sleep but the moment I fell asleep it seemed like my alarm was going off for me to get up for work.

The day flew by because I had a ton of work waiting for me after missing three days. It was one of those days where I didn't really want to talk to anyone so I put on my headphones, blasted my music and focused on trying to catch up with my workload. On my way home I pulled over and stared at my cell phone. *Should I call him?* A part of me needed to know that he wasn't angry with me. I needed to know that he forgave me. I needed to hear his voice.

When he answered he seemed extremely happy to hear from me. I wasn't expecting him to be so welcoming, even after I admitted to him that I lied about where I worked. Tony professed his feelings for me and how much he wanted to change his life. I sat there in disbelief that he wanted to be with me after my disappearing act. I told him how I needed time to figure some things out in my life. I told him I'd be back in touch with him. I was so torn between my feelings for Tony and the love I had for my husband. I must admit it was good to know that he wasn't angry with me because the guilt I was feeling was unbearable at times.

I spent the next day focused on my work and praying. I hadn't talked to anyone, not even Shyla. When she tried to email me at work I told her that I wanted to take some time to myself and that Terrance would be coming by Saturday to talk and I wanted to have a clear mind. Surprisingly, she understood and told me to call her whenever I was ready to talk. That night I had a long talk with God and asked Him to guide my steps.

Terrance and I spent our entire Saturday at home talking. It wasn't the usual *yelling and pointing fingers* type of talking, it was more of a *calm and seeking to understand* type. The talk of divorce seemed to really make him realize that he could lose me forever. There were tears and occasional laughs as we strolled down memory lane. We ordered pizza because we didn't want to leave the house, and spent the evening trying to identify pivotal points in our marriage that caused it to go wrong.

"I think I just became comfortable with you. I forgot the passion we used to have and I looked elsewhere for it. I should've taken control of the situation and gave you a reason to bring that passion back. I let Sherri go and now I have a new male assistant and I realize that the devil places people in our lives to distract us. I was slacking in my business and slacking in my marriage and I blamed everyone except myself. When you said you wanted a divorce, I knew I needed to get right." Terrance proclaimed.

I just sat quietly as he talked. The entire day I contemplated telling him about my affair; I felt so guilty. I wanted to get it off of my chest if we were going to move forward with our relationship but I was afraid of the consequences. I expected a jealous fury to stir up in Terrance and I flashed back to the time when he hit me and the amount of fear I felt. I didn't want to ruin the open connection we were developing that day. I zoned out of his conversation as I frantically battled the *'should I tell him?'* thoughts in my mind.

"Well, are you?" He inquired.

"I'm sorry, Terrance, there's so much on my mind. I didn't hear your question."

"I said that I want to go to counseling immediately. Are you fine with that?"

I sat there quiet for a moment. I needed to come clean with him if we were going to move forward and I needed to put some guidelines in place.

"Terrance, I need to tell you something and I am not sure how to tell you. We've been getting along so well all day and I'm afraid that this will cause a bigger problem."

"Just tell me," he mumbled.

"Well, I….I" I paused as I stumbled on my words. *Have I lost my mind? What he didn't know wouldn't hurt him! But I couldn't move forward unless everything was out on the table.* I went back and forth in my mind, and then I tried it again.

"Terrance, I was very hurt by this whole thing. The only thing I could think about was getting back at you." He put his head down when I said that as if he knew what was coming next.

"I… I want us to go to church together and to go to counseling, but before we do that I need to confess what I've done. Terrance, I met this guy and I slept with him. I didn't intend to sleep with him. I just wanted some male companionship and conversation. I have been feeling so neglected emotionally and physically and it felt good to have a man interested in me. It was a mistake and I felt terrible afterwards because you are the love of my life and I just want to be with you." My hands were shaking as I talked. Terrance didn't react to what I was saying. He just continued to hold his head down.

"Terrance, did you hear me? I slept with another man and I'm sorry. Two wrongs don't make a right and I pray that God forgives me."

"Who was it?"

"Just a guy I just recently met after we argued. I know what you may be thinking but Shyla had nothing to do with it! I met this guy after you hit me and I ended it with him after I slept with him. I know that's not the type of woman I am and I know I am still a married woman."

"Did you use protection?" he asked.

"Of course!" I suddenly flashed back to the condom coming off and felt an uneasy feeling in my stomach. Tony told me he didn't ejaculate inside of me and stopped because he noticed the condom was gone. This morning when I used the restroom the condom slid out from inside me. I sat there on the toilet and cried as I was reminded about the terrible thing I'd done. Terrance and I just sat there in silence and it seemed like forever before he spoke. I waited for this frantic outburst, but it never came. Terrance finally looked up at me with tears in his eyes and said he was sorry.

"Raven, I have always trusted you. I'm so sorry that I put you in that position. I can't stand thinking of you with another man but I'm sorry that I made you feel like that was your only way out. I want us to put our past behind us and move forward. I forgive you, I just really need you to please forgive me. I don't want to lose our marriage."

"I forgive you Terrance, but it will be very hard to forget. I am hoping that God and counseling can help us both forget and move forward. I don't want to lose you. Can we start by going to church tomorrow?"

"Yes, baby, yes! Will I be able to move my things back home after church?"

"Terrance, let's take it one day at a time. Maybe we need to move slowly with you moving back. Let's see how church and counseling goes, ok?"

"Ok. Raven, am I going to have to worry about you going back to this guy when you feel vulnerable again?" He sounded concerned.

"No. I didn't even tell him my real name. I don't want him, I want you. I also want you back home but I think we should wait a few days or so."

For the rest of the day we both ignored our phone calls engaged in deep conversations with each other. It was something I truly missed. With all the stress going on, I almost forgot about my interview Monday morning. Whitters Insurance Companies of Orlando called me earlier in the week to set up an interview with me for the trainer position I applied for. I hadn't even told Shyla and I already knew she would not be happy with the thought of me leaving my job. Terrance, on the other hand, thought it was a great opportunity to make more money and a great way to start things over in life.

I slept in his arms again and he held me tight. The next morning I called Shyla to make sure she and Justin were still coming to church with me as promised.

"Girl, I'm so tired but I'm afraid that if we don't come then you will never let me forget about it," she yawned as she spoke.

"Shyla, I have something to tell you but I won't tell you until we get to church."

"Girl, tell me now! I don't need any surprises!"

"Just be there on time! Bye!"

Terrance and I held hands as we waited at the front of the church for Justin and Shyla. When Shyla got to the front of the church she froze in her steps and held her mouth wide open. I ran to her to avoid her making a scene and pulled her on the side of the church.

"What the hell? Have you lost your mind, Raven?" She seemed very upset as she waited for my answer.

"It's a long story and I promise I will tell you. He's not back at home but we are going to try counseling. Shyla, please don't try to talk me out of this. He's my husband and I love him. I'm not sure if it will work but I want to be able to say that I did everything I could to make it work. I really need your support."

"Fine! I hope you know what you're doing. Let's go find a seat before I change my mind and leave!"

It was friends and family day at the church so it was unusually crowded with unfamiliar faces. As the four of us settled in our seats, I looked around and my heart dropped. I leaned over and whispered in Shyla's ear.

"Oh my God, Shyla, Tony is here!"

"What? Where?" she asked as she looked around.

"Over to the far left." She gasped and shook her head as she spotted him with two women and a child. I immediately prayed that he wouldn't see me. I didn't want to have that confrontation with Terrance here with me. I wondered how he would react if he saw me. He must think I'm this person who sleeps around with men and just dump them. He must think I'm a liar and a cheat. *Was God trying to remind me of the terrible thing I'd done?* I asked God to forgive me again and grabbed Terrance's hand.

"You ok, baby?" Terrance asked.

"Yea, I'm fine. I'm happy you are here with me."

I lost sight of Tony as the church filled up with more people so I breathed a sigh of relief. I tried to refocus my attention on the choir singing and before I knew it I was praising the Lord and forgot all about Tony on the opposite side of the church. Shyla and Justin talked during the entire praise and worship session but I didn't care, I was just happy they were there. I was hoping that Pastor Johnson could touch her soul as he did mine every time I attended church. I felt happy that my husband and my best friend were both there with me because we all needed healing. It just showed that everything happened in God's timing, not ours. He waited until we were all broken so we could get healed together. I had faith that God had an appropriate word for us all through Pastor Johnson and I thanked Him in advance.

The Pastor, Jilah Johnson, had a small afro with beady eyes and a slender build. He looked over the front rows as if he was looking straight through to our souls, and the church became very quiet. Little did we know his words would change the lives of everyone in the congregation that day! He cleared his throat, thanked the choir for a magnificent worship session and began to allow God to speak through him.

"In one voice let's tell the Lord thank you. Get your Bibles out and turn to the book of John. I sense that God wants to reach down into someone's heart and heal it. I want to focus on three different reasons that people may stay away from spending intimate moments with God. Today I want to preach on the topic: *He is God of Your Broken Places.*

Here's a passage I want to share with you, John chapter 3 verses 16 through 18. **16** For God so loved the world that He gave His only begotten Son, that whoever believes in Him should not perish but have everlasting life. **17** For God did not send His Son into the world to condemn the world, but that the world through Him might be saved. **18** He who believes in Him is not condemned; but he who does not believe is condemned already, because he has not believed in the name of the only begotten Son of God.

Condemnation rolls away. There's, therefore, no condemnation to them that are in Christ Jesus who walk not after the flesh but after the spirit. Christ came not to condemn us, not to judge us but that the world through Him might be saved. God sent Him and God so loved us that He didn't just send anybody, He sent his only begotten son. These passages show us that God previewed the condition of the world and the sorrow-filled condition of man. And then, beholding man's sinful condition and lack of regard for His presence and guidance, He still sent Jesus. Paul said, 'While we were yet sinning, Christ died for us; the godly for the ungodly.' So, while we were lost in our sins, God commended His love towards us while we were yet sinners. Jesus came personally for you. If you have a personal devil, then you have a personal Savior. He's so big and so omniscient that He knows who you are and where you are. He's a personal God.

He came to break the curse and to lift man from the despair of the bondages and the things that held him captive. And He came to do it regardless of what caused it and regardless if it was your personal sin, a personal failure, or a bad choice. Do you know how many people are living under a curse that was a result of a bad choice? He's a perfect example of suffering that we should follow in His footsteps. He dealt with those same issues. Jesus didn't come to give you a license to leave your problems and your worries or your cares. He comes to give you power over them.

Whether its demons, devils, divorce, or whatever you found yourself in and however you got there, Christ comes to lift you. So Jesus said that He came to seek and to save *that* which was lost, whether that's your joy, your peace, or whatever *that* is. He came to make you whole. He came to fix everything that was wrong with you. He came to be Lord over all! In order for us to make application of these simple truths that I'm sharing with you right now, you *have* to have faith! All things are possible if you only believe. The message I want for you to get is not only is He God of your whole places and victorious places, but He is also God of life's broken places and He's God of *your* broken places. There are three broken places in our lives.

Number one: When your heart is broken, He's still God. People are hurting all around you right now. People are paralyzed by words that have been hurled like daggers to destroy them. Words have broken the hearts of so many people. People have felt betrayed by the verbiage of the people that they once called friends, loved ones, husbands, and wives, who have now said some things that have shattered their hearts and relationships. People are sitting in here right now lonely in crowds and afraid to share their fears.

Think about the people who are unhappy with their jobs, or the people who are unhappy in their marriage. Think about the people who are paralyzed, even in church, because they feel like in order to serve God properly they need to have their personal life's ducks all in a row. One of the greatest tricks of the enemy is to get saved people to think that God can't use them because there are some situations in their lives that are not together. That's why the Ecclesiastes writer said this, "If you consider the wind, you'll never sow." A translation of that says, "If you wait on perfect conditions, you'll never get anything done." If you had to wait to get perfect before God saved you, you'd still be lost. And if you have to wait until you get perfect before God can use you, you would never do anything for God.

I'm talking about situations when you're overcome by the enemy or when you're living under the residue of all kinds of ills, pains, struggles and strife. I'm telling you right now, you have to let pride go out of the window! You have to die to yourself! You have to be honest and admit to people that you have trouble and you have situations, and you'll never have to get it all together to be used by God. You don't have to have it all together. You may say, "Well, they know my past and they know where I've been," but I say *you* know where you're going! You may say, "Everybody knows what I've been through," but I say that's right, get through it and keep moving. Broken hearts! When your heart is broken, He's still God. We got to understand God. I don't think He ever thinks of us as being dysfunctional when our hearts are broken. When our hearts are broken we need to know that God doesn't see us as unattractive or undesirable. Psalms 34:18-19; **19** "Many *are* the afflictions of the righteous, but the Lord delivers him out of them all."

But the key to that commentary is the verse before it: **18** "The Lord *is* near to those who have a broken heart, and saves such as have a contrite spirit."

Here's another translation: **18** "If your heart is broken, you'll find God right there; if you're kicked in the gut, He'll help you catch your breath."

There is an anointing for broken hearted people. How many times have you looked at somebody and said "Breathe!" I'm telling *you* to breathe, take a deep breath! You're going to be alright because He breathed into man the breath of life and man became a living soul. The devil thinks he can knock the life out of you. But God is right there to help you get life back into you. When your heart is broken, God draws close to you even when you don't feel like you can draw close to Him.

Number two: When your spirit is broken, He's still God. What do I mean by *spirit*? I'm talking about when you've lost your passion, and when you've lost your fire. When you've lost your will to serve God and serve man. When you just feel like giving up and quitting, and throwing in the towel. God is still God. God isn't panicking over your situation. He's not upset that you feel like quitting. The Hebrew writer said, "After you tasted of the heavenly gift and the powers of the world to come, it's impossible." There's no way you are going to be able to walk away from this thing and act like you have never met God. Have you ever met people who used to be on fire for God, who now, all of a sudden, they don't have any joy, any peace, any hope, and seemingly no faith? Have you ever worshipped with people and they're *praising* on Wednesday and by Sunday they have only a little bit of praise? Have you ever asked yourself why certain people aren't *there* anymore? Why they are not doing *this or that* anymore? John says that they go out from amongst us to prove that they were never really of us.

God has you assigned to wherever you are right now, and you are to glorify God wherever you are. God sees you, He knows you, and He knows what you are in need of before you ask. You know that you're better than where you are but that's just where you are. Jesus was better than that cross but that was His assignment in life. People allow the presence of too much stress, unanswered prayers, unresolved problems and people getting on their nerves, as a reason for walking away from God. Ezekiel 11:19-20 says: ¹⁹⁻²⁰ "I'll give you a new heart. I'll put a new spirit in you. I'll cut out your stone heart and replace it with a red-blooded, firm-muscled heart. Then you'll obey my statutes and be careful to obey my commands. You'll be my people! I'll be your God!"

Notice what He did *not* say. He didn't say He was going to fix your old worn-out spirit, He said He'll put a new spirit in you. Some of y'all don't need to re-charge your battery, you need a brand new battery. God's trying to take you to another dimension and to another level, let go and let God. So, if your heart's broken, He's still God. If your spirit's broken and you want to quit, He's still God.

Number three: If your health's broken, He's still God. Health issues are more critical today than they've ever been. If you go to the encyclopedia and look up incurable diseases, there's a list of diseases that the doctors call incurable. People are walking around living in fear of contracting incurable diseases. Not just physical but emotional illnesses as well. Mental issues are plaguing the church that can just be demonic attacks.

Your health condition does not make you useless. I've come to tell somebody that when your health fails, God will not fail. Jesus, in His greatest hour of weakness, knew no sin and became sin. It was at that moment that His purpose for being here was manifested. He was full of disease and if He was going to heal it, it had to be put on Him. It is in His weakness that we are made strong. Isaiah 53:5 says, ⁵"But he was wounded for our transgressions, he was bruised for our iniquities: the chastisement of our peace was upon him; and with his stripes we are healed."

You were supposed to go through what you're going through. He let you go through that thing so when somebody else goes through it you can look at them and say "I'm alive, I made it, I survived, and I didn't give up!!" My message is simply this: He's still God when you're sick, when your spirit is weak and when your heart is broken because He is the God of your broken places.

For the ones who have a broken heart: somebody dumped you, abused you and/or your gifting, somebody took advantage of your generosity, somebody made a commitment to you in a vow and they broke it, and you think you're over it but you're not sure. I want to pray: Father, I pray in the name of Jesus Christ that today will be the day that they mark their calendars as the day in which the healing balm of Jesus came to their house. Lord Jesus, come to their house, heal the broken-hearted, mend the broken-hearted, set them free! In the name of Jesus! Father, we release everybody that hurt us, harmed us, that spoke evil against us, in the name of Jesus! We refuse to hold a grudge, we refuse to be angry another day of our lives. If they would've known who we were they would've never persecuted us, so we release them today and we apply the blood to our hearts. Thank you for our healing, in Jesus name – Amen.

For those with a broken spirit: you lost your joy, you're not on fire like you used to be, you're in every service but you're backsliding, you don't shout like you used to shout, you wanted to walk away. If that's you, let me pray. Father, I pray for renewed strength. I pray, God, that you will create in them a clean heart and that you will put a new spirit on the inside of them. And God, I thank you for it and I believe you're going to do it now, in the name of the Lord Jesus Christ! Just the fact that they've admitted it, God, it's the first step for revival, renewal, restoration and reconciliation. God, I pray that they will realize, Lord God, that there's nothing to give up on and that there's nothing to quit. God, I pray right now that you'll put a spirit of Jeremiah on them and that you'll put fire down in their bones. I break that curse and destroy it and we apply the blood of Jesus to a broken-spirit. Bless them now in Jesus name - Amen.

For the ones with broken health; you have a sickness in your body, or you have a mental illness. Let me anoint you and pray a special healing over your life. Father, I come to you now, standing on the behalf of your people, some sick in their bodies, others sick in their minds. I'm asking you to send your healing angels and your healing word to bring forth wholeness, wellness, renewed strength, renewed joy, restored limbs, restored body parts, renewed vision, and total health. Bind the forces of darkness that have come to plague the physical and emotional bodies of your people. Rebuke cancer, diabetes, high blood pressure, lupus, bi-polar, heart disease, STD's, AIDS, and every other foul infirmity that the enemy has sent to afflict your people. Remove the chains of depression and oppression, suicidal tendencies, schizophrenia, neuroses and dementia. You've not given us the spirit of fear, but the spirit of love, power and soundness of mind. Heal us Lord! Heal us inside and out. I pray it, believe it and receive it, in Jesus name! Amen.

If you have been blessed by this message and you want to accept Jesus Christ as your Lord and Savior, come down to the altar right now. It's never too late to get right with God. If you have already accepted Jesus Christ and you found yourself backsliding and you want to renew your faith, make your way to the altar also."

Before I could grab Terrance's hand, he had already started walking towards the altar with tears pouring down his face. I followed him and held his hand. As I watched the flood of people heading to the altar to give their life to Christ, I saw Tony and one of the women he was with on the opposite end of the altar. Inside I smiled at the fact that he was giving his life to God at the same time I was renewing my faith. I looked to my immediate right and saw Shyla and Justin standing there in tears holding hands. My heart was overwhelmed with joy and I repeatedly thanked God for this overflow of deliverance.

Pastor Johnson stated that everyone could be saved and reborn again by just reciting this statement out loud. "I confess with my mouth that Jesus Christ is Lord and I believe in my heart that Jesus died for my sins and God raised Him from the dead. Please deliver me from my sins and come into my heart."

Chapter Fifteen

Tony: The Daisy

Monica and I met Earlene and my son at the front of the church. I couldn't believe how beautiful Earlene looked, even after all these years. Her butter pecan skin seemed to glow and her long hair flowed like a river. Charles looked like a spitting image of my brother when he was young and I smiled at the fact that he was my son. It had been years since I'd stepped foot in a church, but the moment I walked in it felt like a burden was lifted. The church was pretty huge and filling up with more people by the minute. When we sat down I looked over and saw Monica sitting next to me on one side, along with my son and Earlene on the other side of me and I became overwhelmed with joy. If our relationship would've worked out then that was how I'd imagine it to be. I thought if I ever saw Earlene again that I would be angry but seeing Charles just took away all of my pain. It felt like we were a family and I didn't want this feeling to end.

As the choir performed songs of praise, I sat there feeling grateful for the day. I started thinking over my entire life of deceit with women and felt remorse. I had always believed that everything happened for a reason and now I understood that my encounter with Debra and my run-in with Pastor Johnson were all in God's plan. It was all a way to force me to evaluate my life and to lead me to God. I needed to change my life if I wanted to have any type of happy future.

"Tony, are you ok?" Monica leaned over and whispered in my ear.

"To be honest, my heart is racing and I'm feeling a little light headed, but other than that this is the happiest moment I've had in a long time. Why do you ask?"

"You are sweating and you look a little flushed in the face," she observed.

"I'll be fine. I can see us being the best of friends and I'm happy that you are here.

So, what do you think of Earlene and Charles?" I inquired.

"Aww, thanks for inviting me. Earlene is so beautiful and seems nice. Your son looks just like you, very handsome. I hope to see more of them at your apartment," she nudged my arm as she said that. I turned and looked at them and smiled. Earlene was so caught up in the praise and worship, singing and clapping her hands, that she didn't notice me staring at her. I was looking forward to going off to eat with them after church so I could really get to know Charles. Secretly, I was hoping to get to know the adult Earlene as well. After praise and worship the Pastor welcomed all the visitors and asked everyone to get out their Bibles.

Pastor Johnson's message was entitled *He is God of Your Broken Places*, and I was blown away just by the title. I was definitely a broken man and it just confirmed that it was destined for me to be in that place at that time. I found myself glued to his every word. He talked about having a broken heart, a broken spirit and broken health. His words moved me to the depths of my soul and I knew that it was time for me to give my life to Christ. When he asked for anyone with the desire to be saved to come down to the altar, I immediately stepped out and started walking. Tears ran down my face as I repeated the salvation prayer. I couldn't believe it, I was a saved man. I almost didn't notice Monica standing right by my side with tears streaming down her face as well. We were both broken and in need of healing.

I wasn't sure if it was from the excitement of it all, but my heart started racing extremely fast and I felt a little nauseous so I quickly went back to my seat next to my son and leaned my head on the back of the seat in front of me.

"Are you ok, Tony?" Earlene asked.

"Yes," I whispered. I was trying to catch my breath and could barely speak. I didn't want to let my son see me getting sick so I just continued to lay my head down on the chair. People were starting to leave and I could hear Monica sitting back down and asking me if I was ready to go home.

"I'm going out to eat with Earlene and Charles," I uttered.

"Tony, we can do dinner instead of lunch. You should probably go home and lay down," Earlene sounded concerned.

"Ok, you are right. I may need to go lay down for a while." When I stood up I noticed the room had started spinning so I sat back down. I mumbled a quick prayer to myself, "Lord, please give me the strength to make it to the car," and waited until the room stopped spinning before I stood back up. Monica stood up and put her hand on my forehead.

"Tony, you are burning up! Do you need me to take you to the hospital?"

"No, I'll be fine. I think I was just overwhelmed with everything that happened today. Let's go." I managed to make it to Monica's car and gave my son the biggest hug I could give.

"Son, I know that we just met but I love you. I'm so happy that we were able to connect and I will never leave you, I promise." Charles just smiled as Monica insisted I get in the car. On the drive home Monica started talking about how great she felt about giving her life to Christ. As she continued to talk I noticed myself going in and out of consciousness. Then everything just went black......

When I woke up I was lying in a hospital bed with tubes going in and out of my body.

"How long have I been here?" I asked the doctor standing beside my bed. Nothing had been vivid to me. I turned my head searching for an answer, and I noticed no one standing by my side.

"Can you tell me your name?"

"Tony Wilkerson."

"What year is it, Mr. Wilkerson?"

"It's 1991. How long have I been here?

"A couple weeks, Mr. Wilkerson, a couple weeks. How are you feeling?"

I couldn't believe I'd been there for weeks. I opened my mouth to speak but nothing came out, so I just turned my head and stared out the window. It was a beautiful day outside and I dreaded not being able to run through the trees and lay on the grass the way I used to do when I was younger.

"Mr. Wilkerson, I need to talk to you about your condition," the doctor pulled up a chair and stared at me. Seemed like a thousand moments passed before he said the words that stunned my very being.

"Mr. Wilkerson, are you familiar with a fairly new disease called Acquired Immune Deficiency Syndrome?"

"AIDS? I've heard a little bit about it. Isn't that the disease homosexuals get? I'm not a homosexual."

"At one point we knew very little about the virus and we're still learning more but anyone can be subjected to it, whether you're homosexual or not. Let me explain to you a little about the disease, Mr. Wilkerson. AIDS is caused by a virus called HIV which means Human Immunodeficiency Virus. If you get infected with HIV, your body will try to fight the infection. It will make antibodies, special molecules that are supposed to fight HIV. Being HIV-positive is not the same as having AIDS. Many people can be HIV-positive but don't get sick for many years. As the HIV disease continues, it slowly wears down the immune system. Viruses, parasites, fungi and bacteria that usually don't cause any problems can make you very sick if your immune system is damaged. These are called opportunistic infections. The blood, vaginal fluid, semen, and breast milk of people infected with HIV has enough of the virus in it to infect other people. You can get HIV from anyone who's infected, even if they don't look sick and even if they haven't tested positive yet. Most people get the HIV virus by having unprotected sex with an infected person, sharing a drug needle with someone who's infected, being born when the mother is infected, drinking the breast milk of an infected woman and/or just getting a transfusion of blood from an infected blood donor. Without treatment, the HIV-positive person can contract full blown AIDS. AIDS also includes serious weight loss, brain tumors, and other health problems. Without treatment, these opportunistic infections can kill you."

Before he could finish I intervened, "Are you trying to tell me I have AIDS?"

"Yes, I'm sorry but your immune system has suffered quite a bit of damage and…"

"Just give me the medicine to cure this so I can go home," I interrupted.

"I'm sorry, Mr. Wilkerson, but there is no cure. Your family is out in the waiting room. They are aware that Hospice has been arranged to speak with them."

The doctor continued talking as I zoned him out and looked out the window. I couldn't understand why my life was ending this way and I didn't want to hear any more. As I stared out the window I noticed the daisies in front of the hospital's gift shop outside. I always had this fascination with flowers, particularly daisies. When I was a child I would stare at the daisies in my aunt's backyard. Every day the daisies looked different with the change of the seasons until one day the beauty of the daisies just came to a complete halt. It reminded me of life and the way my life has been. I wiped the tears falling from my eyes as I laid there in amazement.

A Predetermined Lifespan

The life of a flower begins during the bud stage. The bud gradually expands until it is partially open. It continues to expand until the bloom has opened fully. Not long afterward, hours or even minutes, the vibrant color of the flower begins to fade. During the fading stage, the flower starts to lose turgor, a decrease in moisture and vigor within the petal's cells. Cell respiration slows. The flower wilts and begins a slow collapse. Proteins and nucleic acids are lost. Wilted petals may glisten with fluid that has been released from dying cells. Petals and other parts of the flower drop; eventually, the seeds at the base of the dead flower head are ready to be dispersed.

External factors for flower decay can be manipulated so that the bloom of a flower can be enjoyed for as long as possible. The process of flower decay is a natural and necessary one in order for seeds to be released.

Like all life on this planet, flowers, no matter how lovely or vigorous, will eventually begin to decay. The process of flower decay, or aging in general, is called senescence. Vital cells and tissues begin to deteriorate, all because genetic encoding passed on to the embryonic plant has predetermined the duration of its life.

Certain **actions** *can prolong the life of a flower, but the decay process is inevitable. Pollination may actually be one of the triggers for a flower to begin its decline, promoting the endless cycle of life and death in a flower.*

Chapter Sixteen

RAVEN: THE SCENT OF A FLOWER

Today was my last day at the mortgage company. I put in my two-week notice as soon as Whitters Insurance offered me the trainer position. I packed up my desk slowly, reminiscing over every item I packed away. Just my name tag alone took me back to the first time I started working here. Shyla put in a good word for me with her friends over in HR and I just knew I would get the job. On the first day she took me around introducing me to everyone and told everyone to make sure they treated me right. Now I was leaving and it was a bittersweet moment because I had become so accustomed to this place each week, but I felt it was a dead end for me.

"So, you're actually doing it?" I turned around and saw Shyla standing at my desk with tears in her eyes. When I told her I got the new job she didn't speak to me for two days and then treated me to dinner to celebrate. It was hard for her to see her lunch buddy go but deep inside she was proud of me.

"Yeah, I start my new job Monday. I'm so excited and nervous at the same time. What if I don't do well?"

"You will do great, Raven, stop worrying. Do you need me to help you carry your boxes to your car?"

"Only if you wipe those tears from your eyes. This is supposed to be a happy time."

Shyla wiped the one tear that managed to escape from her eye and grabbed one of my boxes. She was such a great friend to me and I would miss going to lunch with her every day. Whitters Insurance was located on the other side of town so having lunch with her wouldn't be an easy task, but we vowed that once I got settled into my new job then we would choose one day out the week to meet half way for lunch. After we loaded the boxes into my car we stood there in silence looking at each other.

"I'm so proud of you, girl."

"Thank you, but we are still best friends. We will still talk every day and I will still come to your house, and you better come to mine! It's not the end of the world, just an enhancement to my world. I love you, girl."

"I love you too, Raven." Shyla gave me one of the tightest hugs I'd ever received and then I headed home to my husband. Life was starting to look up for me and I owed it all to the Lord. When Terrance dedicated his life to God a few weeks ago it made him a new man. He had been to Bible study with me and back to church again. He also catered to me every night, cooking for me and running my bath water. All I could do was pray that God continued to work on him. Maybe we had to go through a storm in order to appreciate the sunshine. That's what trials and tribulations are meant for, anyway, to make us stronger.

Here I was with a better version of the husband I once had, and starting a new job with a position that I'd always desired. My only concern about starting the new job was the fact that I knew I would eventually run into Tony. It was inevitable! What would I say to him? I would be wearing a name tag so he would soon find out that my real name was not Debra Williams. My heart raced as I thought of the encounter and how it would go. I would just have to apologize to him and tell him the truth. I would have to just avoid the area he worked in and let him know that I was happily married. I didn't want to be with anyone other than Terrance but I was also aware of how the devil works; he will use your weakest flaw against you.

I spent the entire weekend lying around watching television with Terrance and trying to figure out what I would wear Monday morning. After trying on four different outfits, I chose my lime green business suit. It was a pencil skirt and a tailored jacket that flattered my figure. I wanted to make a lasting impression because I was so excited about the new venture in my life.

Monday morning I woke up extremely early with a smile on my face. I sat there watching Terrance sleep; he looked so peaceful. I jumped out of bed, got on my knees to say a prayer and then headed to the kitchen to cook breakfast. It had been a long time since I had this much energy in the morning.

"Good morning, are you cooking breakfast?" Terrance yawned.

"Yes, sleepy head, it's almost done. Pancakes, eggs and bacon!"

"Sounds good baby. I'm gonna jump in the shower first," he walked over and kissed me before heading to the bathroom.

I found myself grinning like a little school girl thinking about how much I loved Terrance. I knew that God was still working on him but I loved the beginning stages of what I was seeing in him thus far. After breakfast I nervously drove to my new place of employment. I had butterflies in my stomach as I reported to the conference room. *Lord, please don't let me run into Tony today, I'm not prepared.* When I walked into the room there were three other women and an older man also waiting.

"Come on in. The trainer will be in shortly. She said for us to just wait here and she will be right with us. It's our first day also so I'm sure you're just as nervous as we are," said the tall blonde woman. Her skin was tanned and she had to be at least 6'1" with legs to die for. I just smiled at her and sat there with sweaty palms as I observed the other new hires in the room. The older white man had very pale skin and a thick beard. His suit was slightly wrinkled and he seemed to be in a world all of his own. He stared out the window and seemed to be comfortable keeping to himself. The other two women were young black women and they were both dressed very professional, one wearing a pants suit and the other wearing a dress. They appeared to be friends as they sat there chatting about their nails and where they liked to shop. After waiting for ten minutes, a large black woman walked in.

"Hello, my name is Sheena. I will go over the ins and outs of the company along with our policies and guidelines with you. You will be stuck with me for the first week and then the lead trainer will show you how to do your job the five weeks following. I would like you to introduce yourself and tell us a little about yourself and your work background."

The two young black women introduced themselves first. Sharon and Tamika were both from the same company and had known each other for years. They both were very articulate when they spoke, but I giggled to myself as Tamika spoke because she over-pronounced every word. I thought it was great that they were friends and had a chance to work side-by-side with each other. I found myself missing Shyla and thought how wonderful it would've been for us both to start a new venture together. But Shyla was happy where she was, and maybe it was good for me to venture off on my own from what I used to know. Cynthia, the tall blonde, explained how she was a teacher for ten years but wanted a change in careers and figured training would be the best route for her to go. Steve had worked for different insurance companies since he was a teenager and stated he was eager to start a training position. He seemed to come alive when he talked about all the things he'd accomplished and how much experience he had. His boasting almost came off as a little arrogant but I didn't want to make any pre-judgments. When I stood up I shared my experience working with the mortgage company and how I needed to start a new chapter in my life. I told them how excited I was and that I wanted to learn all that I could and eventually move up in the company.

Sheena was in the middle of telling us about herself when the door opened and a young white lady with tears in her eyes asked her to step outside of the room. We all looked at each other in suspense as we wondered what was going on. Several minutes later Sheena walked back in wiping away her tears and apologized for being so emotional.

"I am so sorry. I just found out one of our assistant managers died last night. Tony Wilkerson was an excellent asset to our company and he will be missed. I'm trying hard to gather my composure."

Did my ears hear right? Tony Wilkerson, dead? My heart started racing as I tried to gather my thoughts. Before I knew it I blurted out, "oh my goodness! I know him! He was a friend of mine. How did he die?"

Sheena walked over to me and whispered in my ear.

"This must remain between only us. He died of AIDS."

My heart dropped! My whole world as I knew it began to close in on me and I felt a shortage of breath. I was intimate with this man and the condom slipped off. What if he infected me? I started to hyperventilate and tears rushed down my face uncontrollably.

"Darling, are you ok? Breathe! Breathe!" Sheena rubbed my back as I tried hard to catch my breath. I couldn't speak. I tried my best to control myself but I couldn't. Tears poured out of my eyes and my heart felt like it was about to jump out of my chest.

"Darling, please go home. I know he was a friend of yours and I'm sorry to break the news of his death to you. Matter of fact, I am saddened by this as well and I think I need to take a day to grasp all of this myself. I'm sending you all home and we will meet tomorrow morning at the same time. Please don't worry, you will still get paid for today."

I managed to gather myself together to walk to my car but my legs felt numb. This couldn't be happening. I felt extreme sadness that Tony lost his life but the thought of me losing mine was unbearable. I sat there in my car crying and thinking about that night I spent with Tony. The note I left Tony that night that stated the night should've never happened felt even more prevalent at that moment. How could I continue my marriage if I'm infected? What if I infected Terrance? I started hyperventilating again and my hands began to shake. I sat in my parked car for over thirty minutes trying to gain my composure. I picked up the phone, dialing my doctor's office frantically, explaining to the receptionist that I needed a same-day appointment. Luckily, someone canceled their appointment and the doctor was able to see me. My doctor's office was twenty minutes away but it felt like I got there in less than ten. When Dr. Smith came in to see me, she looked concerned.

Raven, what brings you in today? You don't look too good."

"Dr. Smith, I need to get a physical and I need a...," I took a deep breath and continued, "I need a test. I need an AIDS test." I held my head down.

"Raven, I can give you one of those tests. Is there any particular reason you desire one today?"

"Doctor, I just found out an old fling of mine died last night. He had AIDS," the words seemed to sound slurred as it came out of my mouth. I must've started hyperventilating again because she started rubbing my back and tell me to breathe! I spent the next hour getting every test and physical that one could get. I wanted to make sure I was completely healthy.

"Ok, the results should be back in a few days. I'll give you a call."

"No! No! Please don't call me. I will make an appointment for Friday to get all of my results."

The next few days were cloudy and everyone's words were hollow. I came straight home from work each day and went to my room, took my clothes off and got under the covers in my bed. Terrance continued to ask me what was wrong but I just told him I wasn't feeling well. It wasn't a lie. I'd felt sick to my stomach ever since Sheena said those dreadful words to me. I hadn't been able to eat and I sat in the conference room every day at work like a zombie. I refused Shyla's calls and just wanted to be alone. By the time Wednesday evening came around Terrance flopped on the bed, took the cover off face and looked at me in concern.

"Ok baby, you need to talk to me. What's going on? Do you not like your new job?"

"My new job is fine, Terrance. I'm sorry, I'm just not feeling well and I just want to be left alone!" I could barely look him in the face when I spoke.

"You have not eaten in two days! Do you need me to take you to the hospital?"

"I ate a little at lunch. My appetite is gone. I have an appointment with my doctor this Friday so I'll see what my issue is. I'm sorry for being so distant. Please just give me this week to rest and clear my mind. I'll make it up to you. Don't worry about me," I kissed him on the cheek and put the blanket back over my face. He sat on the bed for a few minutes in silence and then let out a big sigh before heading to the living room.

My appointment was set for Friday, right after work. When Friday came it seemed like the entire day dragged on and on. I constantly checked my watch and asked to work through my lunch. The closer it came for me to get off of work, the more my heart started to race. In less than thirty minutes I would find out the fate of my future. The drive to the doctor's office was even more nerve-wrecking as I ran a stop sign and almost hit an oncoming car. I had to pull over to catch my breath and force back the tears trying to escape from my eyes.

When I got to the doctor's office, I waited only ten minutes but it felt like an hour. Finally my name was called and my hands began to sweat. Sitting in the room waiting on the doctor seemed like a lifetime. *Why is everyone taking their time?* I thought. When Dr. Smith came in the room she just stood there and looked at me. Tears were running down my face at that time and I thought my heart would jump out of my chest. She walked over and grabbed my hand.

"Raven, I got the results from your AIDS test. The results are..."

To be continued..........

ABOUT THE AUTHOR

Photo by Tyrone Johnson

Angell Marcella Davis was born and raised in Cleveland, Ohio. She now resides in Jacksonville, FL. with her beautiful daughter. She has a degree in Network Administration/Programming and has pursued her writing since her childhood years.

She is the owner and editor of N-to-U Magazine (pronounced Into You), a Christian-based magazine based outside of Jacksonville, FL and surrounding cities. Her writings have won her several awards throughout her lifetime, but the most notable was being the recipient of the 2008 Gospel Announcers Guild Award for Excellence in a Magazine.

Angell considers herself a very spiritual person and believes that nothing is possible without God, so each day she gives thanks for every breath she takes. She has always been a visionary and has a passion for going after her dreams. "Whether I win or lose, I am satisfied with the fact that I tried, and you never fail when you try."

This book, "The Daisy," is her first fiction novel but not her first published book. Her first book, "Removing the Painting," was published in 2010. It is a book of poetry and short stories that will move you and inspire you. Her goal is to become the humanitarian that God created her to be. Be on the look-out for more to come from Angell Marcella Davis.

Printed in the United States
By Bookmasters